P9-AOX-076

# Orphaned Pup

Other Apple paperbacks you will enjoy:

*Underdog*
  by Marilyn Sachs

*Me and Katie (the Pest)*
  by Ann M. Martin

*When the Dolls Woke*
  by Marjorie Filley Stover

*Cassie Bowen Takes Witch Lessons*
  by Anna Grossnickle Hines

*Kid Power Strikes Back*
  by Susan Beth Pfeffer

*Mitzi Meyer, Fearless Warrior Queen*
  by Marilyn Singer

# Orphaned Pup

Eleanor J. Lapp

AN
**APPLE**
PAPERBACK

SCHOLASTIC INC.
New York Toronto London Auckland Sydney

Scholastic Books are available at special discounts for quantity pur-
chases for use as premiums, promotional items, retail sales through
specialty market outlets, etc. For details contact: Special Sales Man-
ager, Scholastic Inc., 730 Broadway, New York, NY 10003.

No part of this publication may be reproduced in whole or in part, or stored
in a retrieval system, or transmitted in any form or by any means, elec-
tronic, mechanical, photocopying, recording, or otherwise, without written
permission of the publisher. For information regarding permission, write
to Scholastic Inc., 730 Broadway, New York, NY 10003.

ISBN 0-590-40885-2

Copyright © 1988 by Eleanor J. Lapp. All rights reserved. Published by
Scholastic Inc. APPLE PAPERBACKS is a registered trademark of Scholastic Inc.

12 11 10 9 8 7 6 5 4 3 2 1                    8 9/8 0 1 2 3/9

Printed in the U.S.A.                                          28

First Scholastic printing, March 1988

# 1

Sara Bradley hopped down from the school bus just behind her little brother, Petey, pulling her winter jacket against her, clutching her books.

The bus door closed with a soft whoosh, and Sara was left to plod up the road after the disappearing Petey. He always churned on ahead, trying to get to the house before she did. These last few days he was worse, sulky and gloomy, like the winter that seemed to hang on forever here in northern Wisconsin. It made everyone snappish — even the bus driver who was usually cheerful.

Petey was out of sight around the bend in the road by the time Sara finally had her books positioned so they kept her jacket partially closed against the chill wind, a wind that had brought afternoon snowflakes.

It was the distant sound of a dog howling that made Sara slow her steps. It came again, more insistent, a crying, and Sara stopped and turned her head in its direction. The cry came once more, plaintive, wailing, fading to an echo.

"Petey! Did you hear that, Petey?" called Sara, running now. The wind pulled at her jacket, and her books slid awkwardly against her arm. The boots her mother insisted she wear made a hollow, clumping sound. "Petey! Petey!" she yelled again.

He was standing in the middle of the road, facing the other way, not looking at her. "What?" he shouted angrily.

"Wait, Petey. Wait." She was out of breath. "Did you hear that?"

"Didn't hear anything," he grumbled, moving off again.

Sara pulled on the sleeve of his jacket. "Just stop a minute, Petey, and listen."

He wouldn't look at her, but stood there waiting with his lips tight and pursed and a scowl on his face, resisting her hold on his arm.

"Petey . . ." she began. "There. There it is again."

The cry of the dog rose high in the wind, loud — as if riding the surge of air — and then it drifted off, dying out to a low wail.

"There! Did you hear it, Petey?" The wind whipped off her hood, pulling her brown hair against her face as she raised her head to catch the sound.

"I hear it. Sounds like a plain old dog to me," answered Petey. "Now, let me go! I want to go

2

home!" He jerked away from her restraining hand.

"Sounds like a dog in trouble, maybe caught in a trap or something." Sara's words were lost, scattered like the snowflakes, with no one to hear, for Petey again started for home.

She dashed forward to catch up with him. "Well, don't you think it sounds like a dog in a trap?" she demanded.

"Don't know. I never heard a dog in a trap and you didn't, either," he finished defiantly, tightening the grip on his lunch pail before he dashed the last few yards to the front step of the house.

Sara followed and heaved a sigh of relief when she saw her mother's Volkswagen in the yard. It meant that her mom was home from the nursing shift and that Sara would not have to care for a grumbling Petey until Al, their stepfather, came home at five o'clock.

That Volkswagen in the yard was also a sign that Sara wouldn't have to take Petey along when she went in search of whatever was making that dog cry. And that she was going to do.

She dropped her books on the hall bench, next to Pete's lunch pail and crumpled jacket. Petey was already in the kitchen munching on something.

Her mother was sitting at the table next to Petey, a cup of coffee in front of her. "Hi, Sara. Cold out, isn't it?"

3

"Yeah, Mom. It's cold," she answered.

Petey moved in with his complaining. "And it's snowing again, just like winter, and then there's nothing to play outside at school and everyone just pushes you and runs around and the teachers won't let you stay inside unless you're sick." He sniffled before he finished the last of whatever he was eating and headed for the TV set.

Her mom sipped the coffee. "Poor Petey. I never should have let him wear his spring jacket this soon. It's certainly not spring today even if it is April."

"Well, I wish you'd let me go without my boots. Libby and Denise don't wear theirs, and they run all over the cruddy school yard in their sneakers with the boys chasing right after them." Sara bit into her cookie, wishing she hadn't said that. Now she sounded just like Petey. According to Al, she was twelve and she was supposed to be smarter. She saw her mother's concerned look.

"And do the boys chase you, Sara?"

"Oh, sometimes," she answered. It was partly true. The boys in her grade only chased Libby and Denise. She was still the "new girl." The fourth and fifth grade boys teased her and she had to pretend it was as much fun as when it was the sixth grade boys, but it wasn't. She missed her own friends back in Milwaukee, the ones she had been with all through grade school. Her mother

4

would only say that it takes time, that things will get better. Sometimes, lately, she got tired of her mother saying these things.

"Sara? Sara?" Her mom was watching her carefully.

"It's okay, Mom. You're right. It's this cold and the weather."

Mom stood up, putting her coffee cup next to the sink. "Al says this last spurt of winter won't last long. It never did when he was a boy."

"I sometimes wonder if Al really remembers how it used to be." That slipped out in a way that Sara knew would cause trouble.

Her mother turned quickly, a hurt look on her face. "Sara!"

"I'm sorry, Mom. But sometimes . . ." Sara left the kitchen and headed for her room before her mom could see the spill of tears. She didn't like this feeling against her stepfather that was growing inside her. Al had been behind this move from Milwaukee to northern Wisconsin, renting this house, saying it was a good place to grow up. Her mom had gone along with it. She said the change was good for all of them.

There was change all right. There was the wedding in July and a new stepfather. There was a move in August to this place, a place that had looked great back then. It had green trees and pretty lakes and lots of vacationers and cabins.

5

But now it was lonely. Most of the neighbors had left for warmer places by the end of fall; a few came only on weekends. It was like a village without people.

The biggest change was getting Al for a step-father. Sara's father had died when Petey was a baby. Sara could remember wishing so hard for a father, imagining the fun they would have. She knew Petey wished for one, too. It seemed to be working for Petey but not for Sara. Maybe she was too old now, maybe it was too late.

Sara changed from her school jeans into her worn, old blue corduroys and pulled on a sweater. She heard the burble of the TV in the living room and Petey bouncing on the couch.

The crying dog. She hadn't said anything about the crying dog and going to look for it. Maybe she'd better not mention it or *Petey* might decide to come along, and he'd just wind up sniffling and grumbling. No. She had enough of that. She'd look for that dog herself.

She grabbed her heavy windbreaker and her stocking cap and mittens from the hall closet.

Her mother appeared in the kitchen doorway, looking surprised. "Are you going out, Sara? What about the weather?"

Sara zipped up her jacket. "That was Petey who was complaining."

"Don't forget your boots."

Sara grimaced but didn't argue as she slid her feet into the ragged boots. She could hear Petey's questioning voice when she slipped out the door. She quickly ran down the road and past the clump of pine trees, making sure she was out of sight of the house and Petey before she stopped to listen.

At first there was nothing, only the wind making whispering noises in the branches. But then she heard the dog's cry, loud and eerie, fading after a moment to a whine. It sounded as if it came from the other side of the main road, from the swamp beyond the cabins.

# 2

Sara ran, her boots clip-clopping, making big splat marks in the snow that was beginning to stick on the road. When she slowed to catch her breath, she listened for the cry. She didn't hear it immediately, but then came a long howl, then a shorter, crying one.

Sara ran past the trailer and the little cabins that were set along the road, down to the end where the road stopped. Here was another empty cabin with a chain across the roadway and a NO HUNTING sign nailed to the tree. There was no one around now, so Sara ran across the yard to the alder brush that marked the swamp and the small stream that snaked through the middle.

There was still an occasional howl and Sara could tell she was getting closer. She was breathing hard from running, and she unzipped her windbreaker a little just before she ducked between the thick alders. They were twisted and gnarled and slippery, with roots sticking up in huge pools of water.

Sara stepped from root to grass hummock to logs, clutching the alder branches to keep from slipping into the creek, which was flooded by earlier melting snow. She balanced herself on a log, just jerking her boot at the last minute from an almost-slip that would have put her in water up to her knees.

Her hat was pulled off by the scrape of a branch as she ducked under a clump of brush. A twig snapped against her face, stinging her cheek.

She heard a yip — a puppylike yip — as she scrambled around an old upended tree that left roots and earth clods poking up into the air.

There! It was a puppy — just a puppy! It was black with a little white V on its throat. It made an uneasy whimper and moved back.

Sara looked around. There seemed to be only one pup and it was not very big and it was not caught in a trap. It looked at her forlornly for a minute before it let out a long drawn-out wail. When it stopped, Sara made a tentative move, holding out her hand, saying softly, "Hi, puppy. That's all right."

The puppy lifted its head and backed warily away and let out another mournful cry.

Sara heard a noise in the brush off to the left and caught a glimpse of another dog. It was not too large; a dingy white with black spots. Then she heard its throaty growl — a threatening growl — and the rustle of brush, and she ran.

Thoughts churned through Sara's head as fast as her feet flew. It's the mother dog. She scared me. Will she hurt me? Sara was almost back on high ground before her foot slipped and she felt her right boot fill with water.

She scrambled up under a pine tree, the thick branches providing shelter from the heavy, wet snowflakes. After she caught her breath, she felt angry with herself. Why had she run? What kind of a scaredy-cat was she? That little pup was crying. The growling dog must have been the mother. She really hadn't gotten a good look at her. And what about that growl? It sounded angry.

Now Sara listened. There was not a yip or a howl. Nothing. There was only the wind blowing through the trees and the snow piling up beyond the edges of the pine.

She whistled the way she heard people whistle for a dog. Then she called, "Here, doggie, doggie. Here, doggie." It sounded silly, but it was all she could think of. She whistled once more.

Sara could feel her foot getting cold where the water had filled the boot, and it made a squishy sound when she moved it. She took a few steps back toward the swamp, but suddenly it looked darker than before, and the snow was sticking in blobs on her jacket and melting on her face.

She would get Al. He should be home, and he would know what to do.

There was no sign of Al's truck when Sara ran up the drive to her house. She burst in, jerking off her cap. "Where's Al?"

"He's going to be late, Sara," her mother answered.

"Oh, just when I need him," groaned Sara.

"What about me?" asked Mom. "Won't I do?"

"It's this dog. The one I saw in the swamp. We've got to go back and find it," said Sara. She saw her mother's puzzled look so she explained about the howling pup and the growling dog and the frantic run.

"I guess you didn't expect me to go because you came looking for Al and you're right. It's getting dark. That must have been the mother dog that growled at you. She probably did that to warn you. She'll take care of the pup."

"But . . . but it was such a tiny pup," protested Sara. "And I really think it needed help."

Her mom went into the kitchen. "You can tell Al all about it when he comes home. He'll know what to do. Now, take off your things because we're just about ready to eat."

Petey was setting the table. "You shouldn't have run away, Sara. If I'd been there with you, I wouldn't have run just because of one little old growl," he proclaimed.

Sara didn't answer. Tonight she wouldn't let him get into what he would have done.

"Anyway," he said, "I think it's Andy's dog."

Mom took the casserole out of the oven. "What makes you say that, Petey? And who is this Andy?"

"Andy Boettcher. He lives down the road and rides on our school bus. I think he has a dog like that."

Sara sat down in her chair with a thump. "Oh, Petey. I think you're making that up about Andy's dog."

"I'm not, Sara!" He curled his lip in a pout. "You always say that to me. I'm not making it up."

"Time to eat," said Mom. "We'll talk to Al about it."


Petey had fallen asleep on the couch, but Sara spent a restless evening looking at the clock and watching the snow steadily coming down in the circle of the yard light outside. It was almost two hours later when the lights of Al's truck flashed against the living room windows.

As Sara rushed into the hall, she heard her mother warn, "Sara, give Al time to get in the door and get his things off."

Sara was looking for her boots. "But we could go right away," she protested.

Al was in the door. "Go where?" he asked.

"To see about a little lost puppy I found in the swamp," answered Sara, trying to keep the pleading out of her voice.

"Whoooa! Now wait a minute. I'm a good two hours late, and I haven't eaten a thing," he said.

"But, Al . . ."

He shook his head. "No, Sara. There's a real snowstorm out there, and I've had a very long day. You can wait a little while longer." He headed for the kitchen.

Sara hung back, reluctantly putting her boots away, hearing her mom's voice in the kitchen. Al was telling her about the terrible slickness on the roads and how tired he was.

Sara went into the living room thinking she should have known better than to ask Al before he ate. He always did things in order, on schedule, in a methodical way. There was nothing to do but wait until he was ready.

She thought about the little black pup out in the swamp. Was that the mother dog nearby, and would she take care of him? It just couldn't be Boettcher's dog. It was too far away.

Al came into the living room and eased into his recliner. "Now," he said to Sara, "tell me all about this lost puppy."

Sara recounted the story again, hoping Al would see how urgent it was to get to the pup quickly.

13

"Sounds to me like that little pup was all right, Sara, if its mother was there," Al said, settling further back into his chair and putting his arms behind his head.

"But, Al, who would the dogs belong to? I've never seen them around here."

Petey was crawling up from the end of the couch, rubbing his eyes and yawning. "I told her, Al. I think the mother is Andy Boettcher's dog. But she never believes me." He went to Al and climbed up into his lap.

Al pulled the sleepy Petey closer. "So you think it's Andy's dog?"

Sara burst out. "He's just making it up!"

"Whooa — now wait a minute, Sara," said Al. "Petey just might be right. He's more aware of dogs than you are. You're the one who is crazy about horses."

Sara pushed back on the couch, with a glare at Petey.

Al moved in the chair, shifting Petey against the other arm. "Now, Sara. I think . . . I think we'll wait until morning. I don't have to be in at work until nine tomorrow, so I'll check on the pup and the mother dog. I can call Boettcher about it and see if the dogs belong to them, as Petey says." Al yawned and hugged Petey. "Most likely if we went back there tonight, we wouldn't even find the mother and the pup. She probably moved him to another spot. Animals do that. That's why you didn't hear any more cries. But I'll check it out tomorrow. That's the sensible thing to do."

Sara knew she wouldn't get him to change his mind tonight. "Maybe we could go early in the morning, before I have to get on the school bus," she said. "I'll get up early."

"I don't know," answered Al. "We may have a problem getting your mother off to work with these snowy roads. And you two have to catch the bus. Anyway, Boettcher should be the one to be worried about the dog."

His last words told Sara there was no use arguing. It was the name Boettcher mostly. Al didn't want to have anything to do with the Boettchers. He never really said it, but she knew he didn't think much of the family down the road. Al had no use for people who always left their yards in a mess and the Boettchers' was really a mess. Sara didn't always want to agree with Al's idea of what looked good, but even she wrinkled her nose when she saw the junked cars and piles of garbage surrounding Andy's place.

Sara's warm bed felt good that night. She thought of the little pup out in the swamp in the snow. She'd ask Al again. She'd try once more in the morning to see if they could go look for the pup before she left for school.

# 3

An impatient Sara watched Al and her mom get the Volkswagen out of the drive and on the main road. Al seemed to take forever as he uncoiled chains, carefully shoveled, and then scattered buckets of sand. Her mom was going to be late for the seven o'clock shift anyway.

When Sara mentioned the dogs, she received a scowl and an angry "Sara!" as an answer from Al. Petey acted up, complaining about everything. Sara's boot wasn't really dry and her toes felt damp as she climbed on the bus, followed by a slow-moving Petey.

The bus crept along on the slippery road to the Boettcher place. Sara saw that last night's snow once again covered the mess in the yard, making strange white mounds out of the junked cars.

No one tumbled out of the big old house. After waiting a few moments, the bus driver moved on. Sara frowned. Now she couldn't ask Andy if that was his dog.

It was Friday and, like most Fridays, it passed quickly. The sun came out around ten o'clock, melting most of the snow. Some of the chicks hatched out in the incubator in Sara's science class, and everyone went in and out of the room all day, admiring the new babies.

The best part was that at the end of the day Sara's mom was waiting. Sara saw the car as soon as she came out of the school building. Petey was already in the front seat, bouncing up and down and eating something. Sara climbed in beside the grocery bags in the back. "Thanks for coming, Mom," she said breathlessly. She had run past the bus line, waving good-bye to Denise and Libby.

Her mom started the car. "I figured you might need a little something special today to cheer you up after last night's storm."

It was when they drove by the Boettcher place, with its ruts of mud and the discarded Christmas tree sprawled on a yellowed snowbank, that Sara remembered the dog.

"I hope Al found the puppy in the swamp," she said, glancing back to see if there was any kind of a dog around the Boettcher house.

Petey turned to Sara. "Andy told me about that dog today."

Sara thumped the back of his car seat with her fist. "Petey Bradley! You're a big liar!"

"I am not!"

"Wait a minute," said Mom. "I came to pick you up so you would be happy. You know how I feel about lying and calling others a liar." She looked in the rearview mirror at Sara.

Sara saw the warning in her eyes. "Mom, Andy Boettcher wasn't even in school today," she explained.

"He was, so!" protested Petey. "He came late. He always comes late. And I asked him about the dog."

Now Sara wanted to know. "Well, what did he say?" she asked.

"He said it was their hunting dog. Someone gave it to them to use for hunting rabbits. But he said the dog never stayed home. It was always running off somewhere. He said his dad is going to shoot the dog if he sees her. He said she might be chasing deer, too."

"Maybe that means we could have her," said Sara. "We could take care of her and the puppy."

"Andy Boettcher says she's no good and his dad knows," declared Petey. "He said there is no puppy, either."

Sara shook her head, her straight brown hair flopping. "Oh, Petey, they don't know everything." But she touched her mother's shoulder. "What do you think, Mom?"

Her mom was making the turn into their yard.

"Don't ask me, Sara. I know nothing at all about dogs or the Boettchers. But Al will know." She braked to a stop. "Now, everyone carry something and we won't have to make any extra trips."

Sara looked for a note from Al when she set the groceries down in the kitchen, but she didn't find one. "Maybe he forgot, Mom. I could call him at the lumberyard and see what he found out."

Mom shook her head. "Not a good idea, Sara. It's all right to call in an emergency when you're here taking care of Petey, but not now. You can wait that hour or so until Al gets home. Besides, Al would have left a note if he had found something. He wouldn't forget."

Petey was already spreading peanut butter on his crackers. "You know what I think? I think maybe Al called the Boettchers and Andy's dad went out and shot the no-good dog," he said.

"Petey!" Mom's voice was sharp. "That's enough of that."

Sara ran into her room to change. She was out in a minute, grabbing for an apple, pulling on her jacket.

"Wait for me," called Petey. "I want to go."

Sara thrust her feet into the boots. "No! You can't go with me!" She didn't want him dragging along, talking about the dog being shot.

This time it was Petey who wailed, but she was

out the door, running down the road. She didn't want to hear any of her mother's ideas about "waiting for Al," either.

Sara had run to the edge of the swamp before she remembered yesterday's growl of the mother dog. She should have brought along something for it to eat. She couldn't take the time to go back and maybe have Petey follow her. The apple from home was still in her pocket but a dog probably wouldn't eat it.

There were no howls, no yips, no barks, or growls. Sara noticed that before she crawled across the swamp puddles, now much higher than yesterday, and crossed the creek. The log bobbed dangerously under her feet.

Her eyes searched the roots and blow-downs, looking for the place she had seen last night. The sun shining on everything made it look different. Yesterday's grayness was gone. Was it that stump? That mound of brush? She couldn't tell. The place that looked like the spot where she had seen the puppy was covered by a big pool of water.

Sara searched for a long time. Water seeped into both of her old boots because she no longer tried to walk on just the dry spots. She tried whistling and calling. Then she walked in a wider circle, up along the opposite bank, peering into any gully or stump overhang, any place where a small pup might be.

Finally she flung herself down on a grassy spot on the hillside, made warm by the spring sun. It seemed that Al was right. The mother dog must have moved the pup. Maybe she would be somewhere in the area.

Sara trudged out of the swamp, but not before she made one more search in the place where she thought she'd seen the pup. This time all she found were her boot tracks, misshapen in the mud, oozing with water.

The search around the nearby cabins went the same way. She found many places she thought might shelter a dog — an overturned boat in one yard, a hole under a pile of scrap lumber, spaces between woodpiles — but all of them were empty. She searched up and down the little roads that crisscrossed the neighborhood. Her searching brought her on the road to Mr. Demmer's house, and she saw his car parked in front of the garage, the trunk open. The shutters had been taken down and Sara could see someone moving in front of the window. She wasn't so sure she wanted to see Mr. Demmer now and take the time for visiting, but maybe — just maybe — he had seen the dog.

Mr. Demmer was a neighbor from April fifteenth to October fifteenth, give or take a few days. That was the way he said it. That was what he told Sara and Petey when he first met them last September. He called Petey "Butch" and told him stories about the railroad where he had worked before his retirement.

A door banged and Mr. Demmer came out, calling and waving, "Hello, Sara. How are you?"

She waved and waited until he came around the car. "Hi, Mr. Demmer. I see you made it back."

He stood with his hands tucked into the coveralls he always wore, making his stout body look even fatter. "We would have been back sooner but we heard about the snow coming, the snow you had yesterday, so we stayed at my daughter's place another day. This sunshine is nice, huh? Say, where's your sidekick — that brother of yours?" he asked.

"He's home. He'll probably be around tomorrow if I tell him you're here."

"Well, you tell him." He busied himself with the boxes in the trunk of the car.

"Mr. Demmer, have you seen a dog around here? One with a little black pup?"

Mr. Demmer looked up with a smile. "What? You've got a dog now, hunh?"

"No, not me," said Sara. "But I saw one yesterday in the swamp, one with a little black pup. Now today I can't find her."

Mr. Demmer shook his head. "Naah, I haven't seen one." He lifted out one of the boxes and held it against the car. "Wait, wait a minute. Last fall, before we left, there used to be a white one that

22

had some black spots — a beagle. She'd come looking for a handout and we'd feed her once in a while. Is that the one you mean? Kind of a wild dog? A stray?"

Sara nodded. "Maybe that's the one."

"But there was no pup. At least there was none in the fall. Maybe she had pups this spring. But, boy, I'd feel sorry for any pups that dog had. I feel sorry for that dog, too." Mr. Demmer picked up the box again. "I think she belonged to that guy down the road, that Boettcher. He doesn't know anything about taking care of dogs. That poor beagle was always hungry looking. I saw her down by the boat landing many times, eating old, rotten fish."

Sara jerked her head up. The boat landing along the lake. She hadn't even thought of looking there because she had seen the dogs in the opposite direction. Now she started to move away, eager to continue the search. "Well, thanks, Mr. Demmer. I haven't looked by the boat landing, yet."

"That doesn't necessarily mean you're going to find her there," he chided.

"No, I know. But I want to look."

This time she ran down the road toward the lake. The pine trees here were tall and thick, shutting out the warm spring sun. Most of the lake was still frozen, but there were small puddles along the shore where it had started to melt. There was a garbage barrel on the edge of the parking lot. Ice fishermen had left bags and cans scattered around, but it wasn't the time of year when there would be much food for a dog to eat.

Sara found the little path that she and Petey had discovered last fall, the one that wound its way in and out of the brush along the lakeshore. There was still plenty of yesterday's snow here, and Sara looked for dog tracks, but she didn't see any. It was the same around the deserted campground, the empty camping spurs and the encircling road. Sara ducked under the gate marked CLOSED and headed for home.

She wished, more than ever, that she had gotten Al to go back and look for the dogs last night. Now they were gone. She certainly hadn't been able to find them anywhere. There was this uneasy feeling that the mother dog might be the Boettcher's dog. But no one else had seen the black pup. And how would she ever be able to convince her family that they should care for them?

Al's truck was in the yard. Sara took a deep breath. She'd just have to try.

# 4

Al called to Sara as she entered the house. "Come on, Sara. We're eating already. You're late."

Late. That didn't help. Al liked to have everyone on time or have a very good reason for not being on time. Sara washed her hands and sat down.

Petey was eating his dessert. "Did you find the dog?"

Sara shook her head. Then she looked at Al. "Did you find them this morning, Al, the pup or the mother?"

Al put his fork down. "No, Sara, I didn't. I really didn't know where to go and something came up and . . . "

He was looking at Sara, and she knew he could see her disappointment.

He scowled. "Well, Sara, I told you the dog wouldn't be there and she wasn't, was she?"

Sara shook her head again, biting her lip. "But maybe . . . maybe if you'd gone this morning . . . "

25

Al swung his head from side to side in an exasperated way. "Sara. You know what kind of a morning it was. We had a hard enough time just getting everyone on their way."

Petey pushed his plate aside. "Andy Boettcher said the dog wasn't any good, and his dad was going to shoot it, and he said there was no pup."

Now Al looked even angrier. "See, Sara? And who wants to have anything to do with that whole mess?"

"But — the little pup — " Sara began.

"No! It's nothing but trouble. It's a mongrel, a cur, half-wild. I certainly don't want to get involved in that mess and certainly not if it's the Boettchers'."

Sara heard it. It was that name Boettcher again. She busied herself with eating, determined not to run away from the dinner table. She barely tasted anything. She was aware of the talk changing to the weather, aware of her mother's voice changing the subject, the peacemaker.

Sara swallowed the food and vowed to herself that she would get involved. She didn't care if it had to do with the Boettchers who weren't as perfect as Al thought they should be. She would wait for the right time, and she would find the pup and the mother dog. Wait. Wait. Wait. It seemed she was always waiting. She was waiting to find the dogs, waiting for spring, waiting for the kids to accept her, and waiting for Al to really become her father. And perhaps — perhaps none of that would ever happen.

Sara did the dishes, swishing her hands in the hot, soapy water, but she was thinking about the dogs. Her mom was busy putting food away, clearing the table, and Sara knew she purposely wasn't saying anything, hoping Sara would "get it out of her system."

Finally her mom spoke softly. "It turns out for the best, Sara. I've said that a lot lately, but it's true."

Sara kept her head down, turning the plate, rubbing the other side.

"Sara? Sara?"

Sara heard the appeal in her voice, the asking for more. "I know, Mom," she answered slowly.

"You have to give Al a chance, Sara. He hasn't had a family before or children. It's hard for him to step in."

"But, Mom, it's not that. It's the dog, the pup . . . " Sara knew her voice had a trembly sound, the sound she'd been trying to keep out of it all night.

"It's not just the dog, Sara. It's your behavior, too." Her mom picked up the dish towel. "This whole lost dog story sounds a little strange. Al has lived in the country, and he feels that, too."

Sara stood very still, not moving her hands. They didn't believe her. They really didn't believe her, and that hurt. She couldn't look at her mother. "Petey heard the pup cry, too, and Mr. Demmer knows about the mother dog. He said so." The tears started to slip out, running down her cheeks, falling into the dishwater.

This time her mom came over and pulled Sara close. "Oh, Sara. I didn't mean to do that. I was trying to help." Her voice sounded shaky. "Sara, Sara . . . I guess it's been a long week or something."

Al appeared in the doorway. "Hey, you two. What's going on here? We're waiting for you in the living room."

Her mom turned and gave Al a weak smile. "We'll just be a minute. We're finishing the clean-up here."

Sara could see the smile reflected in the window above the sink, and she could see Al standing off in the doorway, looking at her mom in that special way. She looked down. Maybe they were right. Maybe the dog was no good or maybe it was gone, back to Boettcher's or someplace else, and the mother dog would take care of the pup. Maybe she just shouldn't think about it.

Mom hung the dish towel on the rack. "Come on, Sara. Empty the dishwater. Let's go in and join the family."

Sara moved automatically, tipping the plastic pan, rinsing it, drying her hands, putting things away. Mom turned out the kitchen light, and Sara followed her.

Al was in his recliner, and Petey was huddled on the couch looking at some pictures in one of Al's outdoor magazines. Mom straightened some cushions before she sat next to Petey.

Sara picked up her library book and stretched out on the carpet next to the fireplace. The TV was turned on low with some kind of comedy on it, but all Sara could hear were the spurts of laughter and not the words people were saying.

Al spoke up. "One of the reasons we moved to the country was so we could have some pets. I was going to wait until we had moved into a place of our own, but maybe we should get a dog now. Petey and I have talked about it. We'd like to get some kind of good breed, one that we could train for something. Right, Petey?"

Petey closed the magazine. "Right! Something like a German shepherd or a black Labrador. This kid in my class has a black Labrador, and he can throw sticks in the water and the dog gets them right away and brings them right back to his hand. He says it's a real smart dog."

Al shifted in his chair. "You have to look at a dog as an investment. You have to pick a good one, with good bloodlines. I'll talk to the customers at the lumberyard. Lots of them have dogs. We might even get a good one without paying too much."

The magazine Petey was holding slipped to the floor. "Will you see about one tomorrow?" he asked eagerly. "Will you ask tomorrow, Dad?"

Dad. Sara heard him say Dad. He did it when he was excited, and she saw that special look come over Al's face when he heard it. She looked back at her book and turned a page, even though she hadn't read a word.

Now Petey was climbing up on Al. "Maybe someone has a St. Bernard," he said.

Al laughed. "Whooa, Petey! A St. Bernard is too big. But I'll start to ask around. We've got time, yet. We don't want to decide too quickly. We've got to make some plans first and get ready. Right, Helen?" He turned toward Sara's mom.

She smiled. "That sounds good, Al. Then maybe after the dog we can see about the horse that Sara has always wanted. That sounds like a good plan, doesn't it, Sara?"

Sara heard her mom, heard the peacemaking, and knew she expected an answer. "Yeah, Mom, that sounds perfect."

Sara looked back at the pages of her book. Too perfect. Al had to have a dog with good bloodlines. He had to have one that didn't cost too much. He had to make plans first. He wouldn't do anything too soon. He didn't care about her or her pup. Sara put her hand under her chin so they wouldn't see it trembling. She'd certainly never make a mistake and call him Dad, now.

The next day was the kind of Saturday morning they'd had all winter. Petey was up early watching his cartoons. Mom was showering in the bathroom and Al was gone, working at the lumberyard until noon.

Sara could tell all these things from the noises she heard as she lay in bed. There was nothing she had to do today, not even watch Petey because Mom was home.

Yes — she had to do something. She had to find that dog and the pup even if she had to walk all the way down to Boettcher's to do it.

If Al could make plans, she could make plans. She had to take something for the dogs to eat, and she had to get away from the house alone to look for them.

Sara climbed out of bed quickly. She put on her jeans and sweatshirt and old sneakers. She took some crusts of bread out of the breadbox and put them into a plastic bag. She pushed the bag behind some jars on the kitchen counter, hiding it until she was ready to go. She fixed a bowl of of cereal for breakfast.

Mom came into the kitchen, pushing back her

damp hair, pulling her robe close. "Sara!" she said in surprise. "You're up and dressed. Did you forget that it's Saturday morning? What's going on?"

Sara finished the last of her cereal before she answered. "I think I'd like to have some time to go off exploring by myself today."

Mom leaned back against the counter. "By yourself, hmmm." She gave Sara a searching look. "I guess that sounds all right." Her words came out slowly.

Sara could tell she was remembering the crying last night. She rushed in. "I mean . . . I've been taking care of Petey a lot lately and I thought . . . well . . . since you were home . . . "

Mom smiled. "Okay. Have a good time. See what's going on, who is here for the weekend, and bring home the news. Al does want to take a ride this afternoon to look at some property possibilities, and I want you to go along with us."

Sara rinsed out her bowl, delaying, not wanting to answer.

"Sara?"

"I'll be back, Mom."

When her mom left the kitchen, Sara tucked the plastic bag with the bread into the pocket of her sweatshirt. She grabbed her jacket and her boots before she went out of the house. Petey was so occupied with cartoons that she wouldn't have to argue with him.

Once on the road, she headed for the swamp. She hurried past cabins and roadways. She stopped to pull on her boots and check her pocket to make sure the bread bag was safe. She had an easier time crossing the log and finding the tree roots because the high water had receded.

Sara did the same careful searching she had done yesterday. She made herself go slowly, peering carefully, listening all the time. Nothing. No sign of a dog or dogs. Maybe it was the Boettchers' dog after all. Now was the time to find out.

She crossed the log again and sat down under the pine trees to remove her boots. She took the bread bag out of her pocket and stuffed it down into one of the empty boots and hid everything behind a woodpile at a deserted cabin.

Then Sara returned to the main road and started off for the Boettcher place. As she walked, she watched for the dogs, looking into the woods, down the logging road, at strange shapes that turned out just to be clumps of brush. The woods looked big — and a dog could be anywhere. She listened, too, hearing the whoosh of cars on a distant road, the squawk of ravens, the chatter of a squirrel in a pine tree.

Soon she was at the bend in the road just before the Boettcher house. She tried not to think about the funny feeling she was getting in her stomach. As she rounded the curve, the hoarse baying of a hound dog came from the tumbledown sheds in back of the house.

A clanking came from the garage behind the junked cars. Sara walked down the driveway, skirting the puddles. Where was Andy? If she'd just see Andy . . .

A man in greasy overalls stood by an engine, tapping it with a hammer. He didn't see her or hear her. She stopped. He kept on turning the rod he was pounding, tapping it. She moved a few steps closer.

The clanging stopped. He looked up — unshaven, rumpled, unfriendly.

"Hi," said Sara. Her voice sounded like a croak. She tried again. "Hi! I'm Sara Bradley from down the road."

"Yeah," he acknowledged, then turned his head off to the side and spit out a stream of brown liquid before he shifted the wad of chew in his mouth. He turned back. "Name's Boettcher. What can I do for you?"

"I . . . I wanted to ask you about a dog you have?" She managed to get it out. "A beagle — I think. That's what Mr. Demmer said it was."

"Yeah. You mean Patchy. That's what we called her." He aimed another squirt of tobacco juice against the oil-spattered sand. "You folks up there in those cabins won't have to complain about old Patchy anymore. I shot her last night. I put her

34

out of her misery. She was just an old bummer. She never stayed home since the folks on the other side of town gave her to me."

Sara's hands curled up tight in her pockets and her heart pounded, but she made herself stand still as Mr. Boettcher leaned against the engine.

He continued in his flat voice. "She must of had pups somewhere, too, from the looks of her. Probably born too early in the cold and died, 'cause she never had them around here. They would have been some worthless mutts anyway. They're better off dead."

He turned back to his machinery. "You tell that old man Demmer, too. I heard him in town once telling somebody I didn't take care of my dogs. Well, now I did. You can tell him so. I just got old Duke, my hound back there by the shed, and I keep him tied up."

Sara couldn't move, couldn't take her eyes off Mr. Boettcher. The mother dog was dead — shot by Mr. Boettcher. But the pup — the pup . . . should she say anything about the pup she had seen?

A door slammed off somewhere and then Andy was there, smirking at Sara. "Sara Bradley! What are you doing here? Did you bring Petey?"

Sara looked at Andy with his dribbles of food down the front of his jacket. "No, I didn't bring Petey."

"Did Pop tell you about Patchy?"

All Sara could do was nod.

Andy stuck his chin out. "I told Petey yesterday that Pop was going to do that. That Patchy was no good, always getting into trouble. And there was no puppy." He moved closer to Sara. "Why didn't you bring Petey over? We could've played army or something."

There was a snort from Mr. Boettcher. "No playing for a while, sonny-boy. You've got some wood to carry in."

Andy made a face and turned up his nose. "Well, maybe when I'm done there'll be time."

Sara started to back away. Her words tumbled out in a rush. "Thanks, Mr. Boettcher. I've got to get going. See you, Andy." She had to run, had to get away from this Boettcher place.

# 5

Sara ran as fast as she could run. She was past the bend in the road before she slowed down. She gave a quick look back. She could no longer see Boettcher's house.

Dead. The mother dog that had growled was dead — shot by Mr. Boettcher. He said she was a bummer. Sara had only had that one small glimpse of Patchy, the mother. But she knew she had seen and heard the pup.

The Boettchers must not know the pup was alive. Mr. Boettcher had said the pups must have been born in the cold and died. But Sara knew that at least one pup must be alive. It must be around somewhere. Why wasn't it crying now the way she had heard it crying the first day?

Sara was back at the road and she found the woodpile where she had hidden her boots. Maybe the best plan was to stay close to the woods where she'd heard the pup before, and if it cried again she'd be nearby. She found a place in the sunshine and sat down to wait, resting her back against a tree.

If she found the pup she could take it home. It had no mother, now. Someone had to take care of it. Al couldn't object to that.

Sara listened. She heard car doors slam and people's voices and the wind stirring in the pine trees. A flock of geese flew overhead, going north, and for a time she heard their steady honking.

She could wait no longer. She had to move; she had to do something. She picked up her boots and started looking again — under the boat, behind the small piles of boards, in a thick clump of evergreens. She widened the circle of her search, trying not to miss any hiding place.

She crossed the road to another yard that had a log-sided cabin and a woodshed and another small shed up on blocks. She was going around that shed when she thought she heard a noise. She stopped, but there was nothing. She took another step. There was a whimper; she was sure of it. She dropped to the ground, peering into the blackness under the shed, but it was quiet again.

Sara moved her hand softly against the ground. She heard another whimper, and this time she made a soft noise in her throat, just like the whimper. And there was an answer from somewhere under the shed.

Sara squirmed closer, making the soft sounds,

calling. She put her hand into the blackness under the shed, against the cold ground. She pulled it back quickly, frightened of that strange feeling.

Now she got up and moved to the other side of the shed and called again, moving her hand carefully along the edge. There was nothing — not even a whimper. She couldn't get under the shed, and she couldn't reach much beyond the edge.

She got up and moved to the third side and cautiously moved her hand further under the building. This time she felt brick and pieces of boards and then . . . something soft. She jerked her hand out. She put it back again to touch the soft thing and she heard a whimper, louder than before, and the soft thing moved.

She pulled her hand out again and sat up. That had to be the pup. Could she get it out? Maybe it would just crawl farther away. She felt again and the soft thing was still there. She moved her hand over it and pulled.

"Owwwwwww" came a loud wail, louder than Sara had ever heard. She held her arm still for a moment, and then pulled again.

Out came a squawling, howling black thing in her hand, twisting and fighting and trying to get away. It was the pup! Sara held fast, pulling him against her, grabbing with her other hand. All this time the wailing and crying went on.

"There . . . there . . . easy, puppy," crooned

Sara, managing now to clutch him in both hands. "Now, now, don't be scared," she soothed. He was bigger than she remembered. He was trying to get away, and he still was howling.

"Shh — easy, puppy," she said gently, pulling the kicking puppy against her jacket.

"Ow — ow — ow." Its head was still jerking and twisting.

Sara sat back against the building, cradling the pup. "Easy, puppy, easy."

Suddenly the movements of the pup slowed and then he lay still. No more howls came; just a few whimpers.

Sara spoke softly. "No mother here. Just me, puppy, just me."

Maybe it was the warmth of her body. Now even the whimpers stopped, and Sara could feel the pup trembling and shaking.

He's probably hungry. That was it. Hungry. If its mother had been killed yesterday, then the pup was surely hungry now. She stood up carefully, holding the pup against her, and went to the place where she had left her boots and the bag of bread. The pup was still quivering. Maybe it would be scared to death. Sara had heard of that happening to wild animals. A boy in class had told about a chipmunk that had died of fright in his hands.

Sara pulled the bread out of the bag, and tore

off a chunk and held it in front of the puppy's nose. "Here — to eat," she said.

The puppy's mouth opened and he grabbed hungrily, tearing at the chunk of bread, chewing and chewing, crumbs falling on Sara's jacket and on her arm. The puppy was frantic, searching for more bread as he quickly gobbled one piece and then another. Half the bread was gone before Sara stopped and put the bag back in her boot.

The puppy licked and worked his tongue and slurped all over her jacket. Sara had to laugh. "You were hungry, puppy. Now I think you need something to drink."

Still tightly holding the puppy against her, she walked toward the woodshed where a piece of plastic covering the woodpile held a little puddle from melted snow. She tipped the puppy's head to the water and he lapped eagerly, his tiny tongue spattering drops and making noises.

She hugged the puppy to her as she went back to the shed where she'd found him. There was a small step on one side of the shed, and the afternoon sun made it a warm place.

Sara sat down and looked at the now-dozing pup. "Pup, little pup," she whispered to the black head across her arm. "I'll bet you were scared out here all alone. You should have a name. I just can't call you pup or puppy. You are an orphan

41

like some of those I've read about. An orphaned pup. O.P. That's it. I'll call you O.P. for orphaned pup."

Now, what would she do with O.P.? Take him home to Al and tell him where she got him — from Boettcher's dog, dead Patchy. Maybe the Boettchers would want the pup if they knew it was Patchy's pup. Sara shivered as she thought of O.P. at Boettcher's place.

Maybe she should wait — for a little while, anyway. She could see what would happen. She could keep O.P. a secret, hidden here somewhere in the settlement. There weren't many people around.

But where would she keep him? He could run and he'd get away, maybe out on the road or back to Boettcher's. She twisted around on the step, bumping the shed door, and it creaked. She moved again, slowly, so she wouldn't wake O.P. The door wasn't locked, so she pushed it with her arm, and it swung a little and then stopped.

Sara stood up and slowly pushed the door open all the way. It took a minute for her eyes to adjust to the darkness of the shed after sitting in the sun. She squinted. High up on the wall was a small window that let in some light. She saw a workbench, like the one Al had in the garage. There was a bundle of newspapers and some boxes, one with dishes and pots and pans sticking out of it. There were life jackets and boat cushions hanging on the wall. A lawn mower stood in one corner.

She could put O.P. in here, for just a little while, until she knew what to do. And what if someone came? But most likely they wouldn't. Not until a weekend — and maybe by that time . . .

Sara turned around in the shed. It was not the best, but she could fix it for O.P. She closed the door so the pup couldn't get out. Then she spread some of the newspapers on the floor. Their neighbors in Milwaukee had a dog, and they always had newspapers spread on the floor.

She moved the boxes to block off the lawn mower and the tools, to keep O.P. away from them. She took an old dish out of the box to use for water and another to use for food. Now O.P. needed a place to sleep. She decided not to use the boat cushions because O.P. might make a mess on them or chew them.

She could bring some things from home. Al had a box of rags in the garage. She would use her jacket to make a bed for O.P. until she brought him something better. He'd like that.

The pup was moving, whimpering, trying to get out. Sara knelt down, talking softly, "There, O.P., easy now, there now." The pup crouched unsteadily for a few minutes before he puddled on the newspapers.

Then he moved around sniffing everything — the boxes, the papers, her jacket, all the corners, the dishes. Sara sat back on her knees and watched, making soothing sounds and talking to O.P.

After he had explored everywhere, he came back to her jacket, burrowing against its lumpiness, moving his legs and tail before he closed his eyes.

Sara had to tell him. "You're an orphaned dog, O.P. No mother anymore. But I'll take care of you, somehow, someway."

There was a belching noise from O.P. before he went to sleep.

The door creaked as Sara pulled it shut. She'd come back later with water and something for a bed and more to eat. For now, O.P. had to be a secret.

She hadn't worn a watch. A rumble from her own stomach told her it must be past lunchtime. And she had told her mother she'd be home for lunch.

# 6

Al was polishing his truck and Sara's mom was out raking in the yard in the places where there wasn't any snow.

Petey was pushing his cars back and forth in the sand in the road. "Here she comes now, Mom," he called. "Here comes Sara. Where were you, Sara? We went without you to see the property."

Sara knew she wouldn't have to answer Petey's questions. He just wanted to tell her things. Her mom was a different matter.

Mom stopped raking and scraped off the pine needles that were sticking to the tines of the rake. "We looked for you, Sara. You said you'd be home. We thought you would go with us," she said.

Sara saw the look that Mom gave Al, the warning one. "I'm sorry everyone," she answered. "I was visiting, looking around. I forgot to wear my watch. It won't happen again."

Al gave the bumper a final wipe. "We missed you, Sara," he said.

Nobody asked about the dog — not a word. And that made Sara sure that she had to wait. Now was not the right time. She held the boots down close to her side so no one would notice them.

All through supper she listened to the things they had to say about the property. Her mom liked the view. Al said it would be an easy place to build, and Petey said it had a neat trail along the lake where he could take his dog.

Dog. Sara sat up a little straighter. "What do you mean — take your dog, Petey?" she asked.

"This morning Dad talked to one of the men he works with and his dog will have pups in a month. I'll get one then," said Petey.

Sara sat very still. "You mean it's all settled already that Petey's going to get his dog?"

Al put down his coffee cup. "Well, pretty sure, Sara. Maybe you should tell her the other part, Helen." He looked over at Sara's mom.

She smiled at Sara. "Al thought — we thought — maybe you'd like a pet now, too. One of the other fellows has some kittens. The horse will have to come later, but how about a nice little cat right now?"

Sara looked straight ahead. "How about a dog?"

"A dog?" Al moved his feet under the table. "We really promised Petey the dog, and the man is charging fifty dollars for the pups, so that's all

we can afford right now. We do want a good dog,"
he said.

"A perfect dog," said Sara, dully.

Her mother spoke up. "Well, I'm not sure you
would say a perfect dog, but nothing's been decided for sure yet. We're still thinking about it."

Not sure — but pretty sure. And meanwhile
O.P. was sitting in that shed. They said it would
be a month before Petey got the dog. She had
some time. She'd get O.P. ready, teach him to do
things so Al would think he was a good dog.

Al and Petey said it was their turn to do the
dishes. Usually that made Sara happy, but tonight
she had planned to get some food ready for O.P.
while she was alone in the kitchen.

Sara read for a while, or tried to, but she couldn't
keep her mind on the story. She kept thinking
about O.P. Maybe he was hungry and howling,
and someone would hear him in the shed.

Sara went out to the garage. She pulled out
several old rags from the box Al used for cleaning.
She folded them up very small and set them by
the side of the building.

By that time everyone had left the kitchen, and
Sara made noises filling a glass with water and
closing cupboard doors before she quickly filled a
small jar with milk. She took out some bread slices
and pushed them into another small bag.

Her mother called. "We're going for a walk

through the campground, Sara. Come with us."

"No, I walked enough today," she answered. "I think I'll just sit around and read." Partly true. That sounded partly true. She had to be careful about that.

When she heard the door close, she stepped into the hallway and watched until they were down the road. Quickly she put on a warmer jacket and grabbed the jar of milk and the bread. She ran around the garage for the rags and stuck them into her pocket.

"Here I come, O.P.," she breathed as she hurried along the road. She slowed her stride so it looked as if she was just out for a walk.

She had plenty of time to get to the shed and back before Al and her mom returned home. She couldn't be caught lying. Petey would have a thousand things to look at and ask questions about and that would slow them down.

She saw the shed across the yard, and this time she avoided all the sandy places where she might leave footprints. The door groaned again and, inside, there were noises from the pup. Sara heard scurrying sounds, as if he was frightened, and then some whining.

She stepped in quickly so he wouldn't get out, and she found him watching her, standing with his legs braced, ready. She knelt down and held out her hand, coaxing. "It's me, O.P. It's me with more food. I'm here."

The milk was not too cold. It had probably warmed up from her body heat as she carried it. As she put the dish on the workbench and filled it with bread and milk, the puppy ran around her feet, making eager noises.

When she put the dish on the floor, the puppy scrambled over the top, pushing the dish, getting his foot in the food. "Wait, O.P., easy." Sara held the dish so he wouldn't tip it over. He gobbled and lapped and pushed against the dish, and when it was empty, he kept licking it, searching for another drop.

His little belly bulged immediately, making him look fat. He wobbled as he took a few steps. Sara had to laugh. "Oh, O.P., you are something."

Now he wanted to play, tugging on the jacket that she had left for his bed, jerking, then retreating, then jerking again. He stopped, distracted by Sara sitting on the floor and he came over, sniffing her jacket, around her back, and her hands.

Just as quickly he flopped down, squeezing himself against her leg, stretching out for sleep. Sara ran her hands along his short black fur. "You like something warm, don't you, O.P.? You miss your mother," she said.

Sara sat that way for a while, letting O.P. sleep, touching him gently, rubbing his belly, talking to him.

She looked up at the fading light outside the window. She'd have to get back home. They wouldn't be gone forever.

Sara pulled the rags out of her pocket, opening them up, bunching them together in a soft pile. She moved her arm carefully, so she wouldn't wake O.P. She'd have to find out more about puppies, what they ate and how to take care of them.

She moved O.P. to the new bed, slipping her hands under him, cradling him with her fingers. He grunted and fluttered his eyelids and quickly curled into a black ball.

Sara stepped out the door to fill the dish with water from the swamp and put it back on the floor, along with the last crusts of bread. O.P. hadn't moved.

There was a coolness in the air as Sara walked home, and she hoped O.P. would be warm enough. Her biggest problem tomorrow would be to get back to the shed. She'd have to have a reason for leaving the house. And she couldn't miss — O.P. depended on her.

She was lucky that night. She was the first one home.

\* \* \*

The house was very quiet the next morning, unusually quiet for a Sunday. Sara climbed out of bed and put on her jeans and her sweater. Maybe it was very early, and she could slip out of the house before anyone was awake.

The kitchen clock showed eight o'clock. Sara found a few scattered breakfast dishes on the table. She walked into the living room and found Al dozing in his chair.

His head nodded, then jerked as he came awake and saw her. " 'Morning, Sara."

"Where's Mom?" she asked.

"Someone called early this morning and wanted to know if she could cover the seven o'clock shift. I got up early with her," he answered.

"That means she won't be back until three," said Sara, more to herself than to Al.

Al stretched and pulled himself out of the chair. "Figured we could have an easy, lazy Sunday, and wait until your mom comes home to see if we want to do anything different."

Ordinarily Sara would have balked at that kind of a Sunday, missing the day with her mom, but today she welcomed it. "That sounds okay," she said.

She made toast and filled a glass with milk, and Al filled his coffee cup and sat down at the table with her. "Petey still sleeping?" she asked.

"Yep. It was all the running around at the property we looked at, and then that long walk last night. I'm bushed, too," Al said. "Maybe I'll just lay back on the couch and read one of my magazines," he added, dumping the last of the coffee into the sink.

Sara, left in the kitchen by herself, hastily finished her breakfast and again prepared some bread and milk to take to O.P. She had to move so it wouldn't seem like she was rushing, but she dared not dawdle too much or Petey might get up and start asking questions.

"Maybe I'll try some jogging along the lakefront," she called to Al from the front door.

"Okay, Sara," he answered.

That was something Sara had noticed once before. When her mom was gone, Al was more easygoing, more relaxed. Maybe having everybody together was hard on Al. Anyway, he didn't ask questions about where she was going or tell her when she had to be back.

# 7

Sara was out of the house and up the road, eager to see how O.P. had spent the night. She fell into a jogging run, one hand held over the milk jar in her pocket to keep it from bouncing out.

Sara heard a car coming behind her. It pulled alongside, and she turned her head to see Mr. Demmer and his wife. Mr. Demmer gave a little toot on the horn, and Mrs. Demmer smiled and waved before they drove off.

In just a few more minutes Sara was in the deserted yard and crossing to the shed where O.P. had spent his first night. Sara didn't hear any yips or cries. But as she came closer she heard scratching and scraping.

She hurried a little faster. It sounded like O.P. was trying to get out. She pushed on the door carefully, listening for the scampers that might tell her O.P. was behind the door. He pushed his way out through the crack, wriggling and sniffing around the step, along the edges of the shed, making little whining cries.

"It's okay, O.P. I'm here," she said. "It's okay, O.P." She knelt down, holding out her hand and the pup circled cautiously, stretching out his neck and sniffing all around Sara.

Sara made herself wait. She really wanted to reach out and grab him but she was afraid that if she missed, O.P. would be under the shed quickly. She knew how hard it would be to get him out. She had to remember that he had been raised in the wild.

Now he sniffed around her pockets, making whimpering noises, nuzzling against her. She laughed. "I guess it's food you want, O.P." She stood up, then, pushing the shed door open the rest of the way.

His rag bed was scattered and tugged in all directions. The water dish was overturned; the newspapers wet and rumpled.

"Oh, O.P., what a mess!" cried Sara.

The pup circled her feet, then followed her inside.

Sara righted the dish and poured in the milk and added the bread. O.P. pushed against her, bumping the dish, and Sara grabbed it just in time or it would have been overturned again.

O.P. gobbled greedily, slurping and sucking and licking and, in no time, the dish was empty and once more O.P. was circling her, sniffing.

"I wonder if I'm giving you enough to eat. You seem so starved." Sara ran her hand along O.P.'s soft black fur. The pup gave a puppy burp and then pounced on one of the rags and began tugging and shaking it. O.P. looked so fierce in his tussle. "So that's what happened to your bed." Sara had to smile as she said it.

She looked around the shed, now cool and dark early in the morning. "I should find a place where you could play outside for a while."

The pup whimpered as Sara turned toward the door. "Hey," she said. "I'm not going anywhere. I'm just going to find a place for you to play outside and be in the sunshine."

She closed the door behind her and looked around the yard. There were some piles of boards off to one side. Maybe she could make a fence but that would take too long. There was a cut-off barrel that was used for a flower planter, but when Sara got closer, it looked like it would be too small for a pup. A garbage can was too tall. Nearby was an old wooden boat that was overturned. If she could tip it over, there would be enough room in there for O.P. to play in without getting away, and she could pull it into the sunlight where it was warm.

Sara tugged on the boat. It was too heavy. She had watched Al turn their boat over many times, but he was a lot stronger. She knew you had to balance the boat just right and then let it down easy, so you wouldn't damage it. She pulled again. She could get the boat up, but then how could she get around to the other side to let it down?

Sara got a board from the lumber pile. This time when she lifted the boat she propped it up with the board, carefully testing to see if it would hold. She had seen Mr. Demmer do this when he had cleaned out his boat last fall.

Now she was around the other side. She tugged and pulled until the boat was up on its side and balanced, and then her arms almost pulled out of their sockets as the boat swung over. She pulled her toes and arms back quickly and the boat settled with a bump.

She looked at it. It was large and had sloping sides that would keep O.P. in, at least for a while.

She ran back to the shed, and again O.P. was scratching and whining, trying to get out. This time Sara knelt by the door as she opened it, and when the pup wiggled through the opening, she grabbed him. He struggled and jerked his head, trying to get away. "It's okay, O.P.," Sara said. "I'm just moving you to a warm place."

She knew she couldn't hold him long and she ran swiftly, the puppy jouncing against her. She set him down in the bottom of the boat and he braced his legs and looked around.

Then he explored, the same way he had explored the shed, looking, raising his nose now and then and sniffing the air. The sunlight streamed across the boat, making it a warm place — except for under the seats where dark shadows lay. After a few more sniffs, the pup lay down in the patch of sunlight and blinked his eyes and settled down for a nap.

Sara smoothed his fur with her hand. He was just like a baby. The neighbors in Milwaukee had a baby, and Sara had watched him eat and nap and play and nap. O.P. was just like that baby. Only the baby in Milwaukee had a mother and a father. O.P. just had Sara.

She wanted to just sit and hold the pup, but she knew he'd have to get used to her gradually. It would take time but she could wait.

Thinking of time made her remember Al and Petey. They might come looking for her. She would say that this was O.P., Patchy's pup, and she found him and she was going to keep him. She could also see Al shaking his head and telling her the pup was not good enough, take him back to Boettcher's.

But she wouldn't. She wouldn't take him back. O.P. would stay here and maybe, in a week or two, she could show them this dog that would be trained. She would show him that he could pick up sticks and walk by her without running away.

And they'd see that he was as good a dog as any fifty-dollar one. As good as any two-hundred-dollar one.

Sara ran her hand along O.P.'s fur again and now it felt warm from the sunshine. He moved and curled up in the opposite direction. She looked at him and sighed. There was so much she didn't know about dogs. She'd have to find out some way.

Sara cleaned up the shed, taking out the wet newspapers and putting them in the garbage can. She took some more papers off of the stack in the shed and spread them on the floor. She left the door of the shed open so the air would warm the inside. Gathering up the rags, she went back to sit by the boat and wait for O.P. to wake up.

Sara sat on the pine needles and leaned up against the boat. Right now it seemed spring might be here to stay. She opened her jacket and pushed up the sleeves.

The ravens were making noises in the treetops across the road. She and her mom had thought the large black birds were crows until Al had told them they were ravens, that crows were only around in the summertime. That was one thing about Al — he did seem to know a lot about animals and told a lot of stories about growing up. He told them to Petey but she listened, too, even though she pretended she was reading. That's when it almost felt like Al was her father. Almost.

Well, O.P. didn't have a father, either. Oh, he had to have a father to be born — she knew that much about dogs — but he probably never saw that father at all. And that father didn't know he was an orphan with no one to take care of him.

O.P. stirred, rolling over lazily in the warmth of the sunshine, and Sara stroked his belly with her fingers. "Lazy puppy," she said.

The pup lay there for a minute, turning a little, stretching his legs.

"You like that, don't you," whispered Sara, and she could tell O.P. was hearing her voice as she saw him turn his head to try to see her.

Then he flipped over, crouching on his feet, nipping and tugging at Sara's fingers. Sara wiggled those fingers. "And now you want to play." O.P. jumped away and then back again, putting his head down, wagging his tail from side to side.

She played with O.P. for a while and then she could tell he was tired again. She put the pile of rags in the bottom of the boat and put her hand by the pile and O.P. curled up, his back against the warmth of her hand. Sara sat that way, with her hand in the boat, leaning over the edge, hoping that the pup would get used to her. Maybe the next time she could hold him in her lap and he would sleep there.

Some noises came from the main road and Sara sat up straighter. She had been so busy dreaming about all the good things with O.P. that she had forgotten to be careful. The noises were coming from people and they were coming closer. Someone was talking. Then she heard running sounds. Suddenly there was the sharp crack of a rifle and then another.

Sara put her hand on O.P. and he jerked awake.

Someone yelled. "You got that one!"

Sara jumped up and grabbed O.P. and the bunch of rags. She raced toward the shed, her heart pounding. She managed to get inside and close the door and then she just stood there, clutching O.P.

She could hear more shouting. "You just nicked that last one! He's around here somewhere. Just let me look. I'll get him." There was a funny, cackling laugh.

Sara had heard that laugh before. It belonged to Andy Boettcher. And who was with him? It had to be his father.

Sara crouched down away from the shed window where she was sure they wouldn't see her. What if they found her with the pup? Would they want it or . . . would they shoot it?

Now she heard several loud thumps, one right after the other. She heard another shout. "Maybe he's hiding around these old buildings!" There were more thumps.

Sara inched her way back to the window. She

could see Andy Boettcher across the road, whacking the sheds with a stick.

What if they came here and hit O.P.'s shed with a stick? What if he started howling? She would never be able to keep him quiet. Sara lay the still sleeping pup and the rags on the floor. She would go outside. She held on to door so it wouldn't squeak and eased herself out carefully.

There were more thumps and the crack of another shot. Then came the shout. "Boy! You got that one this time!" There was more laughter and a snort.

It was Mr. Boettcher all right. Sara had heard that snort yesterday.

There was a rustle of branches and Andy came around the trees, holding a dead squirrel by the tail. He stopped in surprise. "Hey, Sara Bradley! What are you doing over here?" He brandished the dead animal. "See this? Me and Pop are doing a little hunting. I chased this one right out from under the woodshed over there."

Sara closed her eyes and swallowed quickly.

"Just like all the girls," jeered Andy. "Scared of dead things. I bet Petey wouldn't be scared."

Sara tightened her lips. "I'm not scared, Andy Boettcher. Why are you killing those poor little squirrels?"

Mr. Boettcher was suddenly there, holding his

gun. "Hey, girl. Those poor little squirrels, as you call 'em, do some dandy damage. They get in folks' cabins and chew up everything. Best squirrel is a dead squirrel. Right, Andy?" He shouldered the gun and peered up into the trees. "Didn't see no porkie around here, did you?"

"Porkie — that's a porcupine, in case you don't know," announced Andy to Sara.

Mr. Boettcher walked around the yard, past the boat. "We're looking for a porkie that's been chewin' on the cabins. Some folks saw him and told us to get rid of him. Don't want my hound getting over here and getting into one, either."

"Not like Patchy," said Andy. "Right, Pop?"

Sara watched Mr. Boettcher walking around, shuffling in his boots, saw his hand holding the gun. She cleared her throat. "What about Patchy?" she asked.

"Oh, she got a face full of quills from a porkie one time," Andy answered. "Took us a week to pull them quills out."

"Yeah," said Mr. Boettcher. "Should have shot the old bum right then." He stopped next to the shed with O.P. in it. "Well, sonny boy, I don't see that porkie here."

"Hey, Pop. Maybe I should poke under that shed and show Sara how we get the squirrels and chipmunks to jump out." Andy began looking for a stick.

Sara held her breath as she watched Mr. Boettcher.

He shook his head. "Naw. Bring that dead squirrel along. We'll go down the road a-ways and look."

Andy made a final wave with the animal and disappeared.

Sara sat down on the step in front of O.P.'s shed. Her hands were shaking just a little. She moved them to hug her knees and then she just squeezed until all the trembling stopped.

Squirrels and chipmunks and porcupines and poor old Patchy. It seemed the Boettchers shot anything that moved. That would probably include O.P. if they saw him. At least he hadn't moved or made a noise. Maybe somehow he knew there was danger. She certainly couldn't put him outside in a pen now. Who knew when the Boettchers would return.

Sara opened the door and looked at O.P. He hadn't moved since she had put him there. He would have to stay in this shed for a while.

Sara closed the door. She'd better see where the Boettchers were.

# 8

There had been no more shots since the Boettchers had left Sara. There was no sign of their truck along the road. It was as quiet as when Sara had started out in the morning.

When Sara got to her yard, Al was finishing the raking her mom had started the day before. Petey was scooping piles of leaves and pine needles into his wagon.

"Hey, Sara. Dad said you went for a jog by the lake."

"I did, Petey," she answered.

"How come you're coming from that way?" he asked, a frown on his face as he jerked his head in the direction from which she had come.

Sara had to be careful. "I just walked around that way. I took the long way back," she said, as she kept on walking.

"Did you hear the shots, Sara?"

Sara slowed her steps. "Yes, I heard them."

"I think maybe it was the Boettchers, Andy and

64

his dad. We saw them drive by a little bit ago."

Sara edged away. "Maybe," she said. She didn't want to talk about the shots or even think about the close call with the Boettchers.

Petey was backing his wagon toward the woods. "Dad says Mr. Demmer is back, Sara. We should go to see Mr. Demmer."

Sara stopped on the step of the house. "We will, Petey."

Al looked up from his raking. "We ate lunch already, Sara," he said. "Well, kind of breakfast and lunch together because it was so late when Petey got up."

"I can find something," said Sara, opening the door. She didn't even feel funny about Al and Petey doing something together. She had O.P. to do things with.

The first thing Sara did was to hide more food for the pup. She fixed herself a sandwich and hunted through the books in her room. Most of them were horse stories. One had a dog in it but really didn't say much about caring for a puppy.

Then she tried Petey's room and found some dog stories, but they were all the fun kind about boys and their dogs doing something together.

She heard the door bang and then Al's voice.

"We're going to take a break, Petey. There are some good sports programs on TV this afternoon. Your mom will be home in a little while."

65

"Sara!" Petey called. "Sara! Let's go to see Mr. Demmer before Mom comes home." He was at the door to his room. "What are you doing in my room, Sara?" he asked.

Sara didn't answer for a minute. Mr. Demmer had fed Patchy in the fall. He probably knew things about dogs. She knew Petey would tell him about the new dog he was getting and then she could ask all kinds of things about dogs. "Let's go to see Mr. Demmer," she said.

Mr. Demmer was still moving boxes around his garage when they got there, mumbling to himself. "Darn it, you can never find anything around here. It's always packed away in some box or another . . . ."

He would have rambled on and on, talking to himself, but Petey interrupted the mutterings. "Hi, Mr. Demmer."

"Well, hello, Petey and hello, Sara. What brings you out on a fine Sunday afternoon? What, no bicycles yet?" he asked.

"No," answered Petey. "Al said we had to wait a week or so. He has to do some fixing on mine. He said we might have some more snow anyway." Petey sat on the bench in front of the garage.

"We better not have any more snow. It's time for spring, isn't it, Sara?"

Sara was pushing the toe of her shoe in the sand,

making crisscrosses. "I sure hope so, Mr. Demmer. We had enough winter."

Mr. Demmer tucked his hands in the top of his coveralls. "Well, Petey. I know you've got something to tell me, something special, or you wouldn't have come all the way over here on a nice Sunday afternoon."

"Yep, I've got something," said Petey. "I'm going to get a dog, a pup, and we're going to start building the doghouse tomorrow. Al is going to bring the lumber home on his truck."

Sara whirled around. "I didn't know that, Petey — about the doghouse." She hadn't even thought of it or expected it to happen so soon.

Mr. Demmer gave a nod. "Well, Sara, a dog has got to have a doghouse. Right, Petey?"

Petey was swinging his legs on the bench. "And we are going to make a little pen for him, too — just so we have a place to put him when we go fishing or to town or something. Al says we don't want him running around like some of the other dogs around here."

Mr. Demmer bobbed his head up and down. "Yah, yah, Petey, that's the way. You got to take good care of the dog, when you get him."

Sara was trying to get over the shock of the doghouse. She had to think of her O.P. "Mr. Demmer, what else does a dog need?" she asked.

"Good food — something good to eat. Like this," he said, pulling out a small sack of dog food from behind the boxes in his garage. "I fed this to that dog of Boettcher's that was around here, that one last fall. Now I give a little to the chipmunks."

Sara looked at the partly used bag of dog food. That was what she needed. But how would she get that at the store?

"He needs table scraps, too," continued Mr. Demmer. "I always mixed in a few scraps with the food when I had a dog."

"Did you have a dog, Mr. Demmer?" asked Petey.

Mr. Demmer sat next to Petey on the bench. "Didn't I ever tell you about my dog? My Nippers, I used to call her."

Sara sat on the dry patch of grass, hearing bits and pieces of the story, which was a long rambling one, the way Mr. Demmer always told them.

Sara thought about O.P. in the shed and the bag of dog food. She really couldn't ask her mom to get the dog food, and how else was she going to get it? Unless she asked Mr. Demmer . . . and he would probably wonder what was going on.

"Sara? Sara?" Mr. Demmer called her.

"What . . . what did you say?" she asked.

"Did you ever find that stray dog you were looking for, the one I think was Boettcher's?"

Sara tried to remember what she'd said before.

"I . . . ah — no, I didn't find the dog." That was partly true. She didn't find Patchy. Patchy was dead and Boettcher told her that, but she hadn't told anyone else. She had to be careful to keep her story straight; keeping O.P. depended on it.

"Well — just as well," said Mr. Demmer. "Maybe somebody found her and gave her a good home. Sometimes these campers pick up stray dogs and take them home. It would have been the best thing that could have happened to that Boettcher dog."

Petey chimed in. "Andy Boettcher said that dog was no good. He said his dad was going to get rid of her."

"Oooh, is that so?" Mr. Demmer pulled on his lip with a thick finger. "Yah, well, sometimes you have to do that, too."

Sara looked away. She hated the talk about Patchy.

"I'm going to take care of my dog when I get him," said Petey. "Dad — Al — knows all about dogs, and he said mine will be a good one, and he'll help me with him."

Mr. Demmer put his arm around Petey. "That's the way. And what about you, Sara?" he asked.

"Oh, she likes horses," answered Petey.

Sara stood up, brushing off her jeans. "I like dogs, too, Petey. I think we'd better get back. We'll see you later, Mr. Demmer." Sara had to think about that dog food and getting back to O.P.

in a little while. She also had to make sure the Boettchers hadn't returned.

Sara saw her mom's car in the yard. She hung back, letting Petey go in the house ahead of her. Sometimes when she walked in, her mom and Al would move apart and she could tell they had been — as Petey said — hugging and kissing again. Her mom's face would be all smiley and Al would have that kind of funny look on his face. She did notice that Petey didn't grumble about the hugging and kissing quite as much anymore.

She was happy for her mom. But it was one more thing she felt left out of — one more time when their faces were different, and she had to look for her library book and start reading. But now she had something else to do, she could get to O.P.

"Sara." Petey pushed her arm. "How come you don't hear anything, anymore? Didn't you hear Mom?"

Sara looked around. This time they were all watching her. "I guess I didn't," she said.

"I thought we might have an early picnic to celebrate spring. I stopped at the market and bought some hot dogs and buns. Al thought we could walk to the campground and build a little fire. What do you think?" asked her mom.

"It sounds good, Mom," Sara answered. She

could tell by the way they looked that she didn't sound eager enough. "I mean it sounds great. But I've got some homework to do. Maybe I should do that first and then . . . then I'll walk over."

Her mother's smile faded. "Couldn't you do your homework after the picnic, Sara. At night?"

Sara rubbed her hands along the pockets of her jeans. "Well, I could, Mom, but I've been doing some jogging and I'm tired at night. If I do the homework first, it will be all done. You can get the wood and get the fire started and all of that."

Al was looking at her. "We just thought you'd like this picnic, Sara."

Sara nodded her head. "I do, Al — I do."

Her mom moved to start gathering up things. "Okay, Sara. I guess we should be glad you're concerned about the homework. We'll get things ready, and you come over as soon as you can. It should be within the hour, though."

Petey stuck out his lip. "I think she doesn't want to help pick up the firewood. That's what I think."

Al gave him a pretend punch on the arm. "Hey, kiddo, you and I are going to do that, anyway."

Sara went into her room and spread her homework on the desk. She listened to the voices and the laughter and the sounds of packing up. She heard her mom call, "Don't forget, Sara, as soon as you can."

# 9

As soon as the door closed, Sara took some money out of the box in her drawer. She rushed to the kitchen and filled a jar with milk. She set the jar outside by the road and hurried back to Mr. Demmer's house, her hand clamped over the money in her pocket.

She was out of breath when she got to the garage, but Mr. Demmer was still moving boxes around, muttering to himself.

"Hi, Mr. Demmer," she called out.

"Eh, Sara, slow down. You live longer that way." He chuckled after he said it.

"Mr. Demmer . . . could I buy that sack of dog food from you?" Sara asked.

"Hunh? This one? The one I feed the chipmunks with sometimes? Why would you want that? It's half used up."

Sara had to have a reason — a different reason than the real one. "Well . . . you know . . . Petey is going to get a dog, and I want this to be kind of a special present, a start for him."

"Why don't you buy a new bag? A fresh bag?"

"I . . . I need it today. It's kind of special — kind of a quick surprise."

Mr. Demmer tugged on his lip. "Hunh, I see. Well . . . then I'll give it to you for Petey. How's that? I don't want to charge you for a bag that's part empty and part full — whichever way you want to call it." He laughed again. "Here." He held out the bag of food. "You can take it."

"I could buy another one and replace it," offered Sara.

Mr. Demmer raised his hands in protest. "No, no — I'll give the chipmunks some sunflower seeds. They like those better, anyway."

"Thanks, Mr. Demmer. Thanks," said Sara, as she walked out of his driveway. She didn't run until she was out of sight of his house and then her shoes flip-flapped as she sped down the road. She stopped for the jar of milk and shifted the package of dog food to the other arm.

An hour. Maybe she could stretch it a little. But they might get suspicious — or maybe come looking for her. This time there was no scratching at the shed door. Sara set the bag of dog food down and gently pushed on the door. There was a scurrying sound inside and then nothing. She peeked around the door. O.P. was sitting under the counter, by his dish, watching the door and her feet.

73

Then suddenly he pounced, making growling noises, running back to his place under the workbench.

"Oh, O.P. Are you ready to play or are you telling me you're hungry?" she asked.

The pup made the same rush at her feet and scampered back.

Sara set the milk jar on the counter and reached back for the bag of dog food. "I've brought something for you that will make you grow big and strong and into the best dog."

O.P. laid down on the newspapers and watched her. His ears perked up and his eyes were bright.

Sara put some dog food in the dish. Then she poured the milk on top and let it soak for a minute. She'd seen that on TV. She put the dish in front of O.P., and again he gobbled and grunted and pushed and she held the dish so it wouldn't tip over. "I should have called you H.P., for hungry pup," she said.

A pen. That's what Al and Petey were going to build — and a doghouse. Wouldn't O.P. like that? His own house and a pen to play in when he wasn't playing in the yard with her or sleeping by the fireplace while she read a book.

She certainly couldn't build a pen here. There were too many dangers. She had to watch out for the Boettchers and the porcupine.

The boat would have to be the pen for now.

O.P. wouldn't stay in it when he got bigger. And he needed someplace to go to the bathroom. She wrinkled her nose at the puppy droppings that she'd have to clean up.

She just had an hour. This time she put O.P. in the boat and hurried back to clean up the shed. She could hear him scratching and whining. One of the rags from his bed was all wet from spilled water, and Sara took that outside to dry.

When she came near the boat, O.P. stopped scratching and sat listening.

"It's me, O.P. Just me, Sara." When she put her hand down next to him, he jumped away, startled. "Now, don't be frightened," she crooned in her soft voice. "It's only me."

This time O.P. tugged on her sweater sleeve and ran back and forth under the boat seat, bumping his head as he played.

Tomorrow was school. How would Sara ever manage to get here early to feed O.P. before she left for school? She'd have to think of something. O.P. had to be fed at least twice a day.

Sara picked up the pup, and this time he didn't squirm as much or try to get away. Maybe it was that he was just tired or maybe he was really getting used to Sara.

In the shed she found a small box and she put the rags in it and set it on the floor. She laid O.P. in it. "This can be your bed, O.P., and then maybe you won't get everything all wet." She moved the water dish to the other side of the shed. Sara put the bag of dog food up on the bench, out of the pup's reach.

O.P. rolled in the box with the rags, pulling and kicking, making growling noises. Sara rubbed her fingers across his belly. He stopped and lay still, his feet up in the air. She rubbed him again. "Oh, you like that, O.P. You like that, don't you?"

If only she could have O.P. at home, to play with all the time he wasn't sleeping. She gave him a final pat. "I'll have to get over here in the morning. I'll just have to," Sara muttered fiercely to O.P. Then she stepped out and closed the door.

The smoke from the picnic fire drifted through the deserted campground and Sara followed it to the place where Al was giving the fire a stir. Her mom was sitting with her back up against the table, watching Al.

Sara heard his voice. "I can tell she's not happy, Helen."

Her mom answered. "Give her time, Al. It's not even a year yet. My friends told me this would be a hard adjustment for her."

Her. They meant her — Sara. Not happy. She should run right in and shout out what would make her happy. Maybe she should.

No. She wouldn't shout it out. She couldn't. She

didn't know what to say. Right now she'd just better think of O.P. and trying to keep everything smooth until she had that worked out.

Sara turned away and found the small trail that detoured to the beach. She found Petey there. He lobbed stones on the ice that still covered the lake, trying to throw each one farther than the one before.

"Hey, Sara," he called. "Watch me." The stone he threw splattered in the slush and skittered sideways before it stopped. "Pretty good, hunh?"

She nodded. "Pretty good, Petey."

"About time you got here," he said. "We were waiting for you to get here so we could eat. And I'm really hungry."

Sara followed him back up the trail to the picnic site.

The hot dogs were good. Sara found she was hungry, too, and she helped pack up the things when they were through. She thought of what O.P. would do with one of those hot dogs, but there wasn't a scrap left.

Al wanted to walk home along the beach trail. "That lake ice should be going out any day, now, especially with this warm weather, and then it will be fishing time," he said.

Sara remembered the fishing time. They had

all gone out on the lake in the boat last summer. Al had shown them how to fish and even Sara had caught some, and it was fun.

"We'd better get that doghouse built before fishing season, Petey," said Al, giving Petey's hair a tweak. "There won't be much time after that."

Sara kicked against a tree root on the trail. Why did it seem to her that every time she thought of something happy, they had to say something to change it. There was nothing to adjusting to that.

Her mom zipped up her jacket. "That wind blowing across the ice is cool. But you're right, Al. Summer will be here soon and there'll be lots of things to do. And Sara — Al and I were talking. We thought we'd give you a bigger allowance this summer because you're going to have more responsibility at home while we're both working. It would be a good way to start saving for that horse you've always wanted."

If it had been a month ago, or even a week ago, Sara would have jumped up and down and thrown her arms around her mom. Now it came out in a feeble, "That sounds good, Mom."

She noticed that Al had stopped and was watching her, so she said it again, louder this time. "I mean that really sounds good, Mom — Al."

"Hey, what about me?" asked Petey. "I'll need some money to take care of my dog. Maybe I can work for Mr. Demmer. He kind of likes me."

Al laughed. "You'll have to ask him, Petey."

Secrets. Sara remembered a book she had read about secrets and how when you had one secret everything changed. You had to be careful not to reveal the secret and all the while it made other things happen. Sara had that feeling now. For the rest of the walk home she didn't say anything.

Later that evening she was in her room, trying to get her homework done, when there was a knock on the door.

"Sara?" Mom called. "Sara, can I come in?"

Sara stopped writing. "Sure, Mom."

Her mom looked surprised. "But I thought . . . I thought you did your homework before the picnic," she said.

Sara looked at her papers. "Well, I did. But I did have some to finish. I didn't get it all done before." It was partly true.

Her mom didn't look as though she believed that. She closed the door gently and sat on Sara's bed. "Sara, I hope this thing about Petey getting a dog isn't bothering you. You've been such a help to me and such a sensible girl."

Sara didn't say anything. She just shook her head.

"Sara, I know you wanted a horse and we talked about it, but it takes a while."

"That's not it, Mom."

"Then what is it, Sara? We think — Al and I — that something is bothering you."

Secrets. Sara remembered that again. She took a deep breath. "I think things will be okay now that spring is finally here."

Her mom hesitated a minute and then came over and hugged her. "I hope so, Sara. I hope that's it. If there are any problems, I hope you'll tell me." She stepped back. "Now Al made the popcorn and I came to see if you wanted some."

"As soon as I finish this last row of math problems," Sara answered.

Al and her mom and Petey were playing Monopoly when Sara came into the living room. As she munched on her popcorn, she coached Petey until he was ahead in the game.

"Hey, Sara. You have to help me more often. I can be a BW that way," he said. "A Big Winner."

Everyone laughed, including Sara. She had a good feeling that maybe things would turn out all right, secrets or not. She still had to find a way to get out in the morning, to take care of O.P. before she got on the bus for school. Her mom had to be to work at seven and Al had to be there at eight. She and Petey got the bus at seven-thirty. If she got up at six, when her mom did, she could make it. But how could she get out of

80

the house at that time of the morning?

"I'll take your popcorn bowl, Sara," her mom said. "I'm rinsing out the other ones."

Sara handed her the bowl and picked up her library book and found her place.

Suddenly her mom was in the kitchen doorway, holding up the bag that Sara had hidden with the food for O.P. "Who put this bread in a bag and stuck it behind the jars?"

"It wasn't me, Mom," vowed Petey. "It wasn't me."

Now they were watching Sara. "I . . . I put it there," she said. "I . . . I've been putting some bread out for the animals. You know, the animals I see when I've been jogging."

Jogging. That was it. Sara took another breath.

"I want to go jogging before school in the morning. I want you to get me up when you get up, Mom," she said.

"Before school?" Mom was surprised. "That's awfully early, Sara. You'd better wait until after school."

Sara had to think quickly. "It's easier early in the morning. That's when most people jog."

Al spoke up. "She's right, Helen. That is a good time for running. But it is hard to get up that early," he warned.

"I want to try it," insisted Sara.

"Well, maybe I'll go running with you," Al said, as he patted his middle. "I could use some exercise, too."

That was something Sara hadn't counted on. "Who will be here to take care of Petey when Mom goes to work?" she asked. She could see the hurt look on Al's face when she turned down his offer. She didn't look at her mom.

"Well, I guess that's true," said Al slowly.

"Yeah. I need somebody to take care of me, Dad," said Petey. "I'm not going to go running in the morning before school. Not me!"

"I'll stay with you, Petey," reassured Al. "Don't worry." A crooked smile crept across his face, erasing the hurt look.

Sara thought about it when she got in bed that night. Her mom had promised to get her up at six o'clock, but Sara could tell she wasn't happy about it and some of it was because Sara didn't want Al to go along. It would have been fun. Sara and Al, running along in the morning. Just like she'd pictured doing things with a dad, like the ones she had read about. But now there was O.P. She had to think about him first. Maybe later on this summer, after they'd met O.P. She and Al could go running and O.P. could run along behind. . . .

# 10

Sara tried to burrow under the covers but from somewhere came her mom's voice. "Come on, Sara. If you're going to go running before school, you have to get up."

Running? Running? The pup. Sara jumped out of bed.

"It's cool out this morning, so you better put on something warm." Her mom's voice came from down the hall. "And don't forget your watch so you get back in time."

Sara was up and moving fast. She had a lot to get done.

Her mom stood in the kitchen doorway, holding the bag of bread. "I didn't want you to forget this, Sara. Be careful and be back in thirty minutes."

Sara's eyes were still blurry. "Thirty minutes. That's not very long."

"You have to shower if you've been running, and eat, and get ready for school. Now get going."

Sara was out the door, loping toward the road and the shed. Thirty minutes. That was only about enough time to feed O.P. and give him water for the day. She'd have to do the clean-up after school. The bag with the bread bounced in her hand. She didn't really need that for O.P. now, but she would put it in the shed.

Sara pushed on the shed door and surprised O.P., sending him skittering for a corner, wetting all over the paper in his excitement. "Oh, pup. I must have scared you," cried Sara.

Sara filled the bowl with dog food. No milk. She had forgotten the milk. This morning O.P. would have to eat his food with water. She closed the door as she dashed for the swamp and the pools of water.

Then she was running back quickly, the water splashing on her sweater as she ran. O.P. was circling around with his nose in the air, sniffing and sniffing. "You smell food, don't you?" she said. She added the water to the dry food. O.P. was pushing around her legs. She put her hand down, and again he skittered across the floor, peering at her from behind the pile of tools.

She set the dish on the floor and held it. "Come on, pup. Come on, O.P." She looked at her watch and saw that she had fifteen minutes left.

O.P. came quickly at the sight of the food dish. "Your eating habits haven't changed at all," Sara said to him, with a shake of her head. "No matter whether it's bread or dog food. But I don't have to worry about you being too slow that way."

This time O.P. licked out the dish and licked up the wet spots on the floor around the dish. He stopped and then his tiny pink tongue licked her hand. "Hey, that tickles," giggled Sara. "There's nothing to eat there, either."

Again she saw her watch, just ten minutes left. She dashed to the swamp for more water and filled the dish. Maybe after she'd done this once she'd know just how long it took.

Back in the shed, she looked at the newspapers. Quickly she grabbed the messy ones and put them in the garbage can outside. She spread more fresh papers.

She bent down and put the rags back in the box. O.P. was running under the workbench, dashing in and out around her legs. "And that will have to be your exercise for the morning, puppy. I'll be back tonight."

Sara was out of the door and on her way, running hard. She heard her mom's Volkswagen start up, and she met her in the drive.

Mom rolled down the car window. "You're back just in time, Sara," she called. "See you tonight."

Sara waved as the car disappeared. That last dash home had made her breathe hard. Al would really think she had been jogging.

It was hectic but she made it. She just remembered to gather up her homework before Al sent her and Petey out of the house to catch the bus.

Petey was quiet as he stumbled up the road ahead of her. Maybe he was thinking about his dog just as she was thinking of O.P.

Sara looked down the road in the direction of the place where O.P. was hidden. It looked like all the other deserted cabins. Next weekend there would be more people here, getting their cabins ready for the fishing season in May.

All winter Sara had waited for that time. Now she didn't want it to come. She had to have a place to hide O.P., and she had to have more time with him.

The bus pulled over and she and Petey stepped on. No one ever said much on the bus on Monday morning. They were all tired out from the weekend, or maybe they were remembering the weekend.

When the bus stopped at Andy Boettcher's place, Sara opened a book and put her head down, pretending she was reading. She didn't want Andy to see her and talk about Patchy or the dead squirrel or the porcupine. She needn't have worried; no one got on. It looked like Andy would be late again.

School went along the way it always went along with Monday morning slowness. By the time the noon hour came, everyone revived and there was a lot of chattering about what they had done over the weekend. Sara sat with Libby and Denise. Denise did most of the talking, telling about a shopping trip with her mom and sister. Libby's grandmother had come to visit and had brought Libby a new sweater.

Sara just listened. She couldn't tell about O.P. or finding him or any of the things she'd done. Not yet, anyway.

The afternoon dragged on through science and social studies because Sara was thinking of the pup and how happy he'd be to see her.

She had gone into the library during a study time and found a book about dogs. She spent the rest of the hour skimming it. Finally the bus bell rang and everyone was out, banging lockers, grabbing their backpacks.

The waiting buses filled quickly, and Sara looked out the window on her side. There were very few snowbanks left and the first lake they passed had large pockets of open water. There were some large black birds picking and eating things on the ice. And they looked like crows, not ravens. She'd have to tell Al that she'd seen some crows had returned.

Petey and Andy Boettcher sat together on the way home. Sara saw Andy turn around and look at her before he got off the bus. She looked away so he wouldn't say anything.

This time Petey didn't run off down the road for home the way he usually did when they got off the bus. He looked belligerent.

"Andy Boettcher said that Patchy, his dog, was dead. He said that you knew that, Sara."

She answered carefully. "I know that."

"Well?" he asked.

She couldn't tell exactly what he wanted. "Well, what?"

"Well, how come you didn't say something at home about it or when Mr. Demmer asked about it?" he demanded.

"I guess . . . I guess I felt so sad that I couldn't talk about it," she answered slowly. Petey hadn't mentioned anything about the pup. He must have forgotten.

Petey was walking ahead but then he stopped and turned to her. "Andy said something else."

Sara waited, holding her breath.

Petey glared. "How come you didn't tell me Andy Boettcher wanted to play with me?"

Sara let out her breath. "I guess I felt so sorry for Patchy, I forgot that, too." she said.

Petey still looked grumpy, but he seemed satisfied with her answer and resumed walking while Sara walked along side of him. Somehow it was too bad she couldn't take Petey to see O.P. He would like him.

Petey looked sideways at her. "I'm going to tell

Al and Mr. Demmer about Patchy," he said.

"That's okay," she answered. Secrets? No, she couldn't tell Petey yet, either. Later on, maybe later on.

There was a new pile of lumber by the garage, and Petey stopped when he saw it. "Hey!" he yelled. "I bet that's for the doghouse!"

Mom appeared on the step. "So you've seen the lumber. Al had to make a delivery nearby so he dropped this off here. Said he'd surprise you. He wants to start building tonight."

"That's going to be a house for King," said Petey. "I thought about that today. A dog should have an important name. And if it's a girl I'm going to call her Queenie."

"Those sound like good names, don't they, Sara?" asked her mom.

Sara nodded her head. "Sounds good to me," she replied. She was going to be very agreeable now because she had to get out of the house to get to O.P., to see how he survived the day.

"Sara, Al said he'd fix the tire on your bike before he and Petey start the doghouse. Maybe you and I can go for a bike ride while they work on the project."

Sara was getting the dog book out of her school bag. "I really don't need my bike tonight. After the jogging this morning, I'm a little tired." It seemed Sara always had to come up with a different reason for everything lately, and it was making her feel funny.

Her mom looked unsure. "Well, okay, Sara. I thought, maybe you and I could do something, but that's all right." She saw the book in Sara's hand. "A dog book? You brought a dog book and not a horse story?"

Sara set the book on the table. "I thought I should learn something about a dog if Petey's going to have one." That sounded good, and it was true. She wouldn't have to hide the book, either.

Sara dawdled in her room as she changed her clothes. She wanted to dash right out and see O.P., but then she would have to be back for supper. She was making up so many things lately that her mom was getting suspicious. She could tell by the way she looked.

No. Sara had to make herself stay home until after they'd eaten and then, when they were working on the doghouse, she'd get to O.P. and have a longer time with him. He'd be all right until then. She hoped so.

She went back and found some snacks in the kitchen and propped up the dog book so she could do some research while she waited.

She read the parts about dog care and about the dog bed and the training and walking the dog. That seemed fairly easy. She was sure she could do all those things with O.P. Then she got to the chapter on shots and rabies and things that could go wrong and she closed the book. That was too much to think about right now. By the time she was ready for shots she would have to have O.P. right here in her house. She couldn't keep him in that shed forever. Even the dog book said that a dog needed sunshine and fresh air.

Sara tried to get her homework done, but she kept watching the clock, waiting for Al so they could have supper. It seemed like hours. The time dragged and she was sure to have mistakes in her math because she couldn't keep her mind on it.

Petey talked nonstop at the supper table about the new doghouse and Sara was grateful. Al seemed as excited as Petey about the whole thing.

Sara was waiting for everyone to finish eating so she could begin clearing the table. The phone rang and her mother answered. Sara was impatient as she watched her mom nodding and smiling as she talked.

Her smile was even bigger when she returned. "That was Mr. Demmer. They wanted us to walk over for a visit tonight, but when I explained about the doghouse project, Mr. Demmer decided he wanted to come over here and help. So, Mrs. Demmer invited us to come and visit, Sara. I should see her and say hello. How about it?"

Sara was gathering up the plates. "I had planned

to look for some things for my science project. I was going to walk along the lake and maybe through the campground," she said evasively. "I said hello to the Demmers, already, Mom."

Her mom's smile disappeared and Sara didn't watch to see whether she gave Al another one of those I-told-you-so looks.

Al spoke. "You could go with your mom, Sara."

Mom shook her head. "No, that's all right. Sara has seen the Demmers. Mrs. Demmer and I will just catch up on the news." She put the dishes by the sink. "We'll leave the dishes until after dark, Sara. You'll want the daylight for this science project, won't you? What is it?"

"I haven't decided yet, Mom. Mr. Abbert wanted us to look around at different things and decide on something we wanted to observe and study."

At least that was all true. Mr. Albert had made the assignment today, and by the end of the week they were supposed to have a topic.

Al and Petey were already outside, getting the tools out of the garage. Sara heard her mom's call before she left the house. "Don't be too late, Sara."

Then it was a few quick steps for Sara into the kitchen for another jar of milk. This time she took twice as much so she would have some for the next morning. She could hear Mr. Demmer talking to Petey and the clatter of boards being moved. She was out and down the road toward O.P.

# 11

This time Sara could hear whining and scratching and the door bumping and she was sure that O.P. was trying to get out.

She knelt by the door. "I'm coming, O.P. Watch out, I'm coming." As she eased the door open, the black puppy tumbled out, falling down the step, running across the grass. He was dashing frantically around the yard.

Sara was scared. "Here, O.P.! Come here! Come on, O.P.," she called.

It was as though he didn't even hear her and, as she crossed the yard toward him, he ran around the boat and behind the shed. It was as though he was afraid of her. She might never catch him.

Quickly she went back to the shed and got his dish of food ready, bringing it out on the step, calling him. "Here, O.P.! Here! Come here!" There was no sound. She rushed back into the shed for the sack of dog food and brought it out, shaking the bag, rattling it, calling again, "O.P., here. Please come here."

She heard a grunting noise and a bump and soon the pup wiggled out from under the shed, coming quickly to the dish of food.

Sara let him eat for a few minutes and then knelt down and held the dish. He didn't seem to notice her hand as he gulped swiftly.

He was doing the final licking of the dish, when she grabbed him and held him. He was kicking and squirming and she quickly transferred him to the boat and set him inside.

He sat down and looked around and then promptly began playing with a dry leaf that had blown under the seats. It crunched and made scraping noises and O.P. hit it with his paw and picked it up in his mouth. He ended up chewing it and little wet broken pieces fell in the bottom of the boat.

It had been close. She had been afraid O.P. would get away but, luckily, she had thought of the food as a way to entice him. He still seemed half-wild, but maybe that was because he was locked up all day by himself.

O.P. was moving again, chewing on the edge of the seats in the boat, putting his mouth over anything that stuck out and gnawing.

Sara stood up. What else was O.P. chewing on in the shed? She rushed inside. Again the place was a mess, the box for a bed was chewed and overturned. The shovel handle had marks on it and so did an old wooden box under the workbench. O.P. might damage something and then what would she do?

She worked as fast as she could, putting everything she could up high, out of reach. She cleaned up the ragged, wet newspapers again. She found a large pan in the box of old dishes and set that out on the counter. That would hold extra water. It would be easier to fill that at night so she wouldn't have to rush around in the morning.

It started to get dark in the shed and Sara knew the sun must be setting. She went out and this time she climbed in the boat and sat on one of the seats. She had to work with O.P. more so he wouldn't be frightened and try to get away. She held out her hand, making coaxing noises. "Here, O.P. Come on, O.P."

He crouched under one of the seats, just out of reach. She leaned forward, moving her hand, and her foot slid on the bottom of the boat.

O.P. pounced, grabbing her shoelace, growling, tugging, pulling. Sara pulled on the other end of the shoelace and O.P. played, rolling over, sometimes grabbing her fingers.

Finally she could tell he was getting tired and she slipped one hand around his soft body and then the other. He was still squirming, but she placed

him in her lap, talking softly all the time. "Easy,
puppy, easy." She held him tightly at first and
then, as the squirming stopped and the eyes closed,
she relaxed her hold. O.P. gave a final wiggle,
nestling closer to Sara's body warmth.

Now she petted him and stroked his head and
murmured softly. This was how she wanted it to
be with O.P. She wanted him to know her and
trust her.

She sat very still with O.P. on her lap, as the
sun slid behind the trees and the first evening
darkness came. Wouldn't it be nice if she could
just take O.P. and walk home. She could hear
hammering and banging in the distance and knew
that had to be Al and Petey building the doghouse.

She stepped out of the boat, still holding the
pup, who fluttered one eye and twitched and then
burrowed against her arm. She put him down in
the box in the shed. One of these times she wouldn't
have to leave him.

It was getting hard to see in the shed when
Sara stepped out and pulled the door shut.

There was no more hammering. Sara could tell
that as she got closer to her house. There was the
bump of a door and some clatterng and she knew
they must be finished for the night, must be putting things away. She did hear voices.

She saw the doghouse as she came around the

corner. Boy! Would O.P. like that one. His own house, big and square with a nice opening in front. She'd make a sign that said O.P. and put it right above the door.

Her mom was standing by the garage. "Well, what do you think, Sara?" she asked.

"It looks nice, real nice," Sara answered.

Peter and Al came out of the garage and Petey put his hands on the doghouse. "See that, Sara? It's almost ready for King. And we made a roof that lifts off, so we can clean it easily. Mr. Demmer thought of that. It just needs a few more things and we're done. Right, Dad?"

Al nodded. "That's right, kiddo."

"And I told Dad and Mr. Demmer about Patchy," said Petey.

Sara looked up cautiously. "Oh . . ." she said.

"How come you didn't say anything, Sara? How come you didn't tell us?" asked her mom.

"She said she felt sad about Patchy," answered Petey.

Al picked up the hammer. "Sometimes those things happen to dogs and other animals. But Boettcher should have taken better care of her. She was nothing but a tramp dog."

Sara pushed the toe of her sneaker against the garage floor. She couldn't say anything. She wanted to say that she had O.P. That he wasn't a tramp dog. But she'd have to wait.

"And where's the dog food?" demanded Petey.

"What?" asked Sara.

"The dog food," he repeated.

Mom stepped forward. "Mr. Demmer wanted to know where the dog food was that you were going to give Petey." She was watching Sara.

Sara saw the real doubt in her eyes. She stopped moving her toe. "Well . . . I hid it. I wanted it to be a surprise."

Al had the funny frown on his face as he looked at Sara.

She continued quickly. "I was waiting until Petey had the puppy, that's all. I have it hidden away."

Petey peered at her. "You could give it to me now."

Sara shook her head, feeling trapped. "No, I couldn't, Petey. I don't have it here. It's hidden."

Al still had the frown. "Why would you do that, Sara?"

Mom hesitated a moment before she put her arm around Sara's shoulder. "I guess that's all right, Sara. I suppose you wanted it to be a real surprise. Petey's waiting for the dog, and I guess he can wait for the dog food, too."

It was like one of those maze puzzles, this secret thing. Everytime Sara did something she had to find a way out of it or turn around. She wondered if she would ever get through it. This time her mom had saved her with her peacemaking, but there was something different about it, something she couldn't quite understand.

The pup. Mr. Demmer must not have remembered the pup, either. If Sara hadn't seen the pup and remembered him no one else would have. Then what would have happened to him? It was bad enough about Patchy, but now that she knew O.P., had held him, stroked his black fur, felt his pink tongue. . . . She couldn't let anything happen to him.

Her mom had turned on the yard light and Al had closed the garage door on the new doghouse, saying, "I'll leave my truck outside tonight."

Everyone got ready for bed early and Sara reminded her mom to wake her at six o'clock. Sara was glad she had done her homework earlier. The getting up early had made her tired. She took the dog book to bed with her but turned off the light after only two pages because she couldn't keep her eyes open.

# 12

It was Tuesday morning and Sara was out and on her way to O.P. Everything had worked perfectly yesterday so she felt she had a good routine started. There was not a cloud in the blue sky and there was a smell in the air that just had to be spring.

The only thing that made Sara uneasy was thinking of how her mom had been unusually quiet as she had gotten ready. Her mom hadn't had much to say at all, but Al, on the other hand, had been too cheerful.

Sara pushed the uneasy feeling aside. She checked her watch; it was time for O.P. Would he be in the shed this morning? She wouldn't have time to look for him the way she had last night. She'd have to remember to leave an extra amount of food. Maybe he was getting out because he was hungry.

She pushed on the door. He was there, sitting on his bed of rags, watching her. That sitting lasted only a moment. Then he was running around, pushing, jumping, until she put his feed down.

Sara did the quick clean-up while he ate. Maybe she could run around outside with him for just a short time to give him some exercise. She checked her watch. It was too risky.

She did squat down and rub O.P. and hug him before she left. "I'll be back tonight, O.P. Mornings go fast, but I'll have time tonight."

O.P. whined, the kind of whine Sara didn't hear much anymore. It sounded sad and lonesome. She hugged him again. "I'll be back," she promised.

Sara was out of the yard and on the sandy road, before she saw the strange, little animal. It was just a little bigger than O.P. It didn't run away but it moved along slowly.

Sara was up to it quickly. Now she saw the small head with the beady black eyes and the body that was covered with quills. It had to be a porcupine.

It continued along with its side-to-side waddle, but it turned slightly when Sara came closer, as if to protect itself. This must be the porcupine that the Boettchers were looking for. It looked like a harmless little creature. Then she remembered Andy's words about Patchy having a face full of quills. She could see the quills all right. It looked like this animal had thousands of them. It kept moving down the road, never turning around.

Sara looked at her watch. She was ten minutes late now. She had thought she had everything right. What would her excuse be? She'd tell them about the porcupine, and that wouldn't be an excuse.

Sara's mom was not quiet as usual when Sara walked in the door. Her words tumbled out. "Sara! You are pushing it! You know the morning schedule around here."

"Mom, I saw this porcupine this morning, right in the road. . . ." Sara's words trailed off. They were all looking at her in a strange way.

It made her feel defensive. "I did see one! And it's the one the Boettchers were looking for on Sunday."

Al was suddenly curious. "What do you mean the Boettchers were looking for it on Sunday?"

Sara felt trapped. Things were becoming a jumble. She couldn't remember what she had said before. She licked her lips. "Well . . . on Sunday I saw the Boettchers and they were looking for a porcupine they were going to shoot." She stopped.

"Go on!" Al's voice was sharper. "I'm sure there's more. You didn't tell us that the other day. You just said you heard shooting."

"I did." Sara hesitated. She looked at her mom, who was clearly waiting for more. Sara put her head down. "They were looking for this porcupine and shooting squirrels."

"And where were you when this shooting was going on?" demanded her mom.

"I was . . . I was out walking around," Sara mumbled.

"Is that when they shot Patchy?" asked Petey.

"No!"

This time even Petey looked angry. "You don't know, Sara. You don't know that for sure. Did you see it? Did you?"

"Okay, Petey, that's enough," said Al.

Her mom jumped up. "Look at that clock. It's time for me to go to work." She turned back to Sara. "We'll talk about this tonight."

"But, Mom — "

"Not now, Sara. It's just too many things, like this being around the Boettchers when they're shooting. You'd better get ready for school now." Her mom picked up her coat. "And you'll have to take care of Petey after school. I have a dentist's appointment after work."

She was gone. Sara felt more than uneasy now. Her mom had been grim and had forgotten all about the peacemaking. If Sara only hadn't stopped to watch that porcupine. . . .

"Petey, you get moving," said Al. "You, too, Sara."

Sara hung back. "What do you know about porcupines, Al?" she asked.

Al looked at her. "I know a lot. Why?"

103

"Could you tell me some of those things?"

Al exploded. "Sara! You're something! You come in late, you get this whole house in an uproar — and you want me to tell you about porcupines. Get a move on so you can catch that bus. Make the porcupine that great science project you're always talking about."

Sara fled to her room. What had she worried about earlier this morning? That he had been too cheerful? What a laugh! If Petey had asked about something he would have gotten one of Al's great stories.

There were strained good-byes when they left the house for the bus.

Sara had time to think about the morning when she sat in math class. It was the first time since her mom married Al that Sara had seen her really angry. Mom and Al had been different in the morning, too, before she had run to see O.P. Maybe they had a fight. Maybe they were fighting about her. Maybe they were fighting about her "adjustment." That made her feel uncomfortable.

That feeling stayed with her all day until science class. Mr. Abbert took all of them to the library to do some research. He wanted them to have that kind of background before they decided on their project.

He came to Sara's table. "How about you, Sara? Are you close to any decision?"

Sara had been sitting there thinking about dogs and squirrels and what Al had said this morning about making porcupines her project. She looked up at Mr. Abbert. "How about me studying the porcupine?" she asked.

"Good idea, Sara!" he answered. "Now, look for some things here. If you have any questions, just ask. Maybe I can help."

Sara found several books with information about the porcupine's habits, its living patterns, and about its quills. Some of the things she read about animals and porcupine quills were scary. That's when she sought out Mr. Abbert.

"Just how does an animal — say a dog — get a face full of porcupine quills?" she asked.

"A dog, or any animal, is usually curious about this slow-moving creature. He may put his nose close to smell it and wham, the porcupine hits the animal with his tail full of quills."

Sara shuddered. "But how would you get them out of a dog?" she asked.

"You have to hang on to the dog and pull those quills out with a pair of pliers. You have to be sure to pull them straight out. The quills have tiny little barbs on them and they hurt. Best way is to keep your dog away from porcupines." Mr.

Abbert nodded to Denise who was raising her hand. "Someone else needs me, Sara. You've got a good start."

Sara had just enough time left to check out the books before the bell rang.

Sara had the seat to herself on the bus ride home. She had lost this morning's uncomfortable feeling, but she knew she still had this thing to work out with her mom. She was sure she could work it out.

Petey jumped out of the bus and was only a few steps ahead of Sara, when she heard the howl. It was the crying howl she had heard last week, the first day she had seen O.P. Only now it was closer and it was louder. It had to be O.P.

Petey stopped. "Did you hear that, Sara?"

Sara started walking toward home very fast. "No, I didn't hear anything. Hurry up, Petey." She was almost running.

"Sara, wait," Petey called. "Listen!"

Sara didn't wait, and she didn't listen, and she still heard the cry again. It was definitely O.P. howling and he had to be in trouble.

"Petey, you're imagining things. Now hurry," she said as she went up the steps.

"Sara, what's the matter with you?" cried Petey. "Why are you saying those things?"

Sara didn't look at him. "Petey Bradley. Stop

being a crybaby. I'm in charge tonight. You get right in the house and turn on the TV and have something to eat. I've got a lot of homework."

Petey went into the house. "Okay, Sara. I'll do what you say, but I'm going to tell Mom."

Sara held her breath. She had to get him in front of the TV before she ran back to see what was wrong with O.P., and she had to do that before anyone else heard the pup. She made herself wait in the kitchen while Petey found the crackers. She waited a few minutes more after she heard him turn on the television.

Then she slipped quietly out the door. Petey wouldn't move for a while, and by that time she was sure to be back. She had to be back before her mom returned. She heard the wail of O.P. and she ran as fast as she could.

The shed door was open and Sara knew he wasn't inside. Another wail came from out in back by the woodpile where Sara found O.P. squeezed into a corner. He looked at her and backed up and wailed again. He acted just like he had in the swamp, the first day she had seen him.

Sara moved closer and saw a thing sticking out of the side of his nose. It was grayish and thin like a twig, and it didn't move or fall off as he whined and moved away.

Sara held out her hand and said, "Come on, O.P. Come on puppy." She knelt down.

Now she saw the thing on his nose clearly. It looked like a big gray needle. O.P. brushed at the thing with his paw and howled again. It had to be a quill from that porcupine. She saw another one and another one. How many more quills? She should have gone back and double-checked the door after she saw the porcupine this morning. She should have — O.P. howled again.

What was it Mr. Abbert had said? Use a pair of pliers and pull them out.

Sara ran back to the shed and found a pair of pliers on the workbench. She was back before O.P. had a chance to make another one of those horrible howls. He still pulled away. She had to catch him and hold him. She crept closer on her hand and knees as he whimpered and pressed against the woodpile. She grabbed for his leg and jerked him toward her. He howled and cried and whined and struggled. She held fast, pulling him backward between her legs, holding him there. She accidentally bumped one of the quills, and he cried out again.

She was panting now, as fearful of all the noise he was making as she was of the quills in his nose. She picked up the pliers. She put one hand on the side of his head to hold it still and worked the pliers with the other hand. Mr. Abbert had said to pull it straight out. She pulled quickly, like pulling off an old Band-Aid. One quill was out, held by the pliers. She brushed it off and gripped the second one. It came out quickly. The third quill was shorter and she had to fumble with the pliers before she grasped it. O.P. was still as she gave the final jerk.

They were out. Were there any more? She couldn't see any. O.P. gave a whimper and then he turned and licked Sara's hand. She dropped the pliers and pulled him into her arms. "Oh, O.P., I got them out. They must have hurt terribly. They were right in your nose."

O.P. didn't even wiggle. Sara hugged him again and held him close. All of a sudden it seemed that the world was very still and very quiet. Sara wondered if anyone besides Petey had heard the terrible howling. And where was the porcupine? Sara peered into the trees and looked around the yard, but there was no sign of it.

Sara took O.P. back to the shed and fed him. He ate slowly, not pushing his nose way into the dish. "Poor O.P. You've probably got a sore nose. It will get better," she said. He didn't move about much, and Sara was sure he was tired. *She* certainly was. She had to get back home to see about Petey. O.P. would be all right for now. She also had to think of some way to secure that door so O.P. wouldn't get out.

Her mom was home when she got there and Petey had told her everything. Sara could tell that

109

by the set of her mom's mouth as she said, "Sit down, Sara!"

There was not much hope of working things out now. Sara slid into the chair and waited.

"Sara, I asked you to take care of Petey, and I come home to find you gone and he's all alone. Then you come in with your school clothes all dirty. This morning we heard how you had been around the Boettchers when they were shooting. You didn't tell us that before. There are so many things going on and so many things you're saying . . . I'm angry about all of it. You go to your room, now. There'll be more later when I get a chance to talk to Al."

Sara was hardly up out of the chair when her mom whirled around. "And when I say talk to Al — that means we're a family, Sara. We'll decide together."

After all the troubles with O.P. and the quills, Sara couldn't find the energy to say anything. She changed her clothes and fell sound asleep until her mother called her for supper.

There was light chatter from Petey all through the meal. It was as though he wanted to avoid trouble. He had all kinds of things to say about school. He even volunteered to do the dishes with Sara.

When Mom and Al went into the living room, Petey asked, "Did you go to find the dog, Sara?"

She didn't look at him. "No," she answered in

110

a way that let him know he had better not ask any questions.

When the dishes were finished Sara went into the living room to hear the pronouncements she was sure would be coming.

They came from her mother. "Sara, we've decided to ground you after school."

Sara thought of O.P. when she asked, "For how long?"

"We're going to do it for one day at a time, starting today," answered her mom. "We think that there is something you are not telling us. If and when you do tell us, we might change our rules. Do you want to tell us that something now?"

Sara shook her head. She needed just a little more time. O.P. would probably be all right and sleep tonight, but tomorrow . . .

"I can still go jogging in the morning before school, can't I?" she asked.

Her mom looked at Al. "We didn't — "

He finished for her. "We didn't discuss that time in the morning. I think we should let her go running, Helen. The grounding after school stands."

Her mother agreed. "And don't forget, Sara, when you are ready to tell us . . ."

Sara excused herself, saying she had homework to do. She wanted to get back to O.P. to see if he was all right, but she would have to miss tonight. He probably had been running and howling a long

111

time with the porcupine quills. Maybe he would just sleep.

This time it was Al who stopped in before bedtime. "Sara, you asked me this morning about porcupines. Is there anything special you want to know?"

Now Al was sounding like the peacemaker, the one to smooth things over. There was something about the way he stood there that made her change from the no that she planned to give. "Yes, Al. I'm doing this research about dogs getting into porcupine quills. Mr. Abbert told me how to get them out. Then what happens? Does the dog get sick?"

Al considered for a moment before he answered. "It all depends. If it's a lot of quills, a dog might get sick. The ones I've seen just had a few and they seemed to be all right. Anything else?"

"Do dogs get porcupine quills more than once?"

Al smiled. "Some dogs learn right away to stay away from the little critters. Some tackle a porkie every time they see one."

Which kind of dog would O.P. be? Sara had that to worry about. She saw Al, still standing there. "Oh, thanks, Al."

"Glad to help, Sara. See you in the morning."

# 13

No one called her — Sara was sure of it. She opened her eyes and waited and listened. There was noise in the kitchen and she could hear Al and her mom. Everything seemed very dark; it couldn't be six o'clock yet. Sara turned on her lamp and fumbled for her watch. It said 6:05.

Sara climbed out of bed and put on the old jeans and sweatshirt for running. Maybe her mom had forgotten. But it seemed so dark, darker than yesterday. Maybe her watch had stopped.

She stumbled toward the kitchen, yawning and stretching.

Mom was making breakfast. "Sara, I didn't call you because you can't run today. Something's come up."

Now Sara was awake. "What do you mean I can't run? You said last night that I could run before school." She looked at the kitchen clock. It said 6:10.

Her mom slid the eggs onto a plate. "It has

nothing to do with last night. Al just had a call from the lumber company. A big truck came in early and they want him to get there as soon as he can to unload — before it rains."

Sara sucked in her breath. "Oh, Mom. I have to run. I'll be back in twenty minutes. I'll be back before you leave. I promise." She started putting on her sneakers.

There was a clatter from the frying pan as Mom set it down. "Sara! You can't go running this morning. There's a storm coming, a rainstorm."

Sara jerked on a knot in her shoelace. "I can't miss, Mom. I'll be back in fifteen minutes."

Mom turned down the radio, already crackling with static. "No, Sara! Not this morning. This is getting ridiculous!"

Sara squeezed her eyes shut. "Mom! I have to go," she said, trying to keep from crying. She had to get to O.P. He had been all alone since yesterday, since the problem with the porcupine.

"Now what?" asked Al, coming into the kitchen.

Sara shook her head, and she saw her mom press her lips together. The kitchen clock said 6:15. There was not much time left for O.P.

Her mom slumped against the counter. "She wants to go running, and I told her she couldn't this morning because of the rain, and you are leaving — and we need her."

Al looked at Sara. "Let her go, Helen. Maybe

she needs to get wet. It won't hurt her. Just be back at six forty-five, no later, Sara."

Sara was grateful. She was out the door when she heard his last words. "You baby her too much, Helen."

Those words made her run faster. Baby her. The only one they ever babied was Petey, either one of them. Petey this and Petey that. Petey gets a dog and Sara, you be sensible, you help out, you are grounded. . . .

It was dark and Sara could hear the distant rumble of thunder. She'd be back in time. She didn't want to get wet, and she hated to be outside in thunderstorms.

A car rushing past on the main road even had its lights on. Her watch said 6:20. She'd make it.

Sara sped across the grass toward the shed. This was going to make her a faster runner. None of the boys would catch her now — if they ever chased her.

Sara stopped. The shed door was open! "O.P.?" she called. "O.P.?" She ran into the shed. As dark as it was she could see that the bed was almost like she had left it last night. There wasn't any mess. "O.P.?" she called.

She should have done something about that door last night. She should have been able to come back after that trouble with the porcupine.

She ran outside. "O.P.! — O.P.!" She flung herself down and peered under the shed. "O.P.?" Her watch showed 6:25.

She ran back in the shed and grabbed the sack of dog food and ran out into the yard, rattling it, shaking it as she had done before. "O.P.?" she yelled.

She ran to the boat, looking in it and around it. The bag of dog food bumped against her leg. "O.P.?" She ran to the woodpile where she had struggled to get the quills out.

She heard Al's truck leaving the house, slowing, then turning down the main road and fading off in the distance. She looked at her watch — 6:35.

Now she widened her search, around the cabin, near the edge of the woods, calling frantically, rattling the bag. He would come bounding out any minute. Sara was sure of it. The rumbling thunder was coming closer. Now she could see a lightning flash far off, and it seemed to make the sky even darker.

She ran back to the shed, dropping on her knees and calling. O.P. just had to be here, somewhere. He had probably been out all night. 6:40. She had to go back. Her mother had to leave.

Sara left the bag of dog food in the shed, and she left the door open and she ran home, faster than she had ever run before. She didn't want to get into more trouble. She'd come right after school, whether she was grounded or not.

She heard a car horn tooting. That was her mom tooting for her.

"Sara! That's too close. Petey is watching out the window. I have to go now or I'll be late. Watch the clock, Sara. I'll be here after school."

The car chugged off and Sara saw the lights come on. It was getting dark, dark as night. There was a boom of thunder and the crack of lightning was close.

Petey was at the door, looking worried. "I don't like these storms, Sara. How are we going to get on the bus?"

Sara didn't even want to think about the bus. All she could think of was O.P. He was somewhere out there. He would be out in this storm, and this was really going to be a storm.

Petey was close at her heels. "You'd better get ready, Sara. Mom said it wasn't long until bus time. She made me turn off the TV because it was storming."

Sara sat at the kitchen table. O.P. She should stay and find him. She had to. The storm might frighten him even more, make him run into the woods and be lost forever.

Petey came to stand by the table. "Sara, aren't you going to get ready for school?"

The kitchen clock said 7:00. Sara went into the bathroom and washed and brushed her teeth. Petey came and stood by the door.

"It's awful dark out, Sara," he said.

There was a loud bang of thunder.

"Did you hear that, Sara?" he asked in a scared voice. "Did you hear that? I wish Al didn't have to go to work so early this morning. Sara?"

Sara came out of the bathroom. "It's just a storm, Petey. It's one of those rainstorms." She said it as much for herself as for Petey. She wanted Petey to stop talking so she could think about O.P.

"Al said it's supposed to turn cold after this rainstorm. We might even get some snow. Al said he heard the weather report on the radio."

Sara rushed to her bedroom, exasperated by all his talk. "Don't you ever say anything without saying Al — Al said?"

Petey's lip trembled. "I'm scared, Sara. I'm . . . I'm . . ." and he started to cry.

Sara grabbed him and hugged him. "It's okay, Petey. I'm sorry. I'm scared, too."

Petey sniffled. "Why don't we stay home, Sara. Let's say it's raining too hard to go to school."

Sara let go of Petey. She could. She could say it was storming and Petey was scared. They wanted her to be responsible and not be a baby. Her mom wouldn't like it if they missed school — but she was in trouble anyway. Then she could find O.P.

Petey was pulling her arm. "Sara? What's the matter?"

"Just thinking, Petey, just thinking," she answered.

"You think the bus driver is waiting for us?"

Sara shook her head. "Not yet."

"It's awful dark, Sara."

She could tell them how scared Petey was and how he wanted to stay home. There was another loud boom of thunder and a nearby crack and the lights went out.

Petey started crying. "I'm scared, Sara. I'm scared." He came and held on to her, clutching her.

Sara was scared, too, but she tried not to let it show. "It's just the lights, Petey. The lights went out. They'll probably go back on any minute. That's okay."

"Is it raining yet, Sara? Is it raining?"

Sara looked down at Petey who had buried his head against her so he wouldn't see the lightning. "No, it's not raining yet, but it's going to — any minute. The wind is really blowing. Come on, Petey, look."

"I don't want to look, Sara."

The kitchen was dark, the clock face dim in the gray light and Sara could see it said 7:10 — the same as it had before. Of course. The clock had stopped when the electricity went off.

Petey pushed up against Sara. "I bet that Andy Boettcher stays home today."

"He probably will, Petey," she answered. She thought of the Boettchers and Patchy and O.P. She had promised to take care of O.P., and now he was out in this storm.

There was a heavy rushing and swirling and the rain came, loud and hard, spattering against the windows and drumming against the roof.

There was a thump up above. Petey jerked his head in alarm. "What's that, Sara?"

"Probably a branch from one of the trees, hitting the roof," she answered.

"Did the bus go yet, Sara?"

"I don't know, Petey. I think it probably did."

"And are we going to stay home?" Petey took a few steps toward the window. "Boy, it's really raining. I hope it doesn't turn to snow. I'd rather have rain than snow. And the thunder is going away, isn't it, Sara?"

Sara was heading for the closet, looking for her raincoat.

"You're not going to get on the bus, are you Sara?" asked Petey, alarmed again.

Sara was tugging on the raincoat, thinking of O.P. "No . . . I thought I'd go outside and make sure everything is all right."

"I'm coming, too." Petey started looking for his raincoat.

Sara hadn't thought about that. What would she

do with Petey? He wouldn't stay in the house by himself, not during a storm, not after the trouble yesterday.

Mr. Demmer. She'd take Petey over to Mr. Demmer's and then somehow she would get back to look for O.P.

"Put on your raincoat, Petey. I'm taking you over to Mr. Demmer," she said.

"Hey, that's a good idea, Sara," said Petey. "I'd like it over at Mr. Demmer's." He was eager now, sliding into the yellow slicker. "I'm going to tell Mr. Demmer about the lightning and thunder and that the lights went out."

"His lights will be out, too, Petey," she said, pulling up the hood of her coat, tying it.

The rain still came in gusts and torrents as they stepped outside and big streams ran down the road and into the ditches. There were broken branches scattered everywhere.

It was colder. Sara noticed that. It was like a winter cold. Where was O.P.?

Petey walked along without saying a word, his head bent to keep the rain out of his face.

Sara slowed at Mr. Demmer's driveway. She'd have to leave Petey there and then be sure to get away. She could see Mrs. Demmer in the big window in her bathrobe, pointing at them.

Mr. Demmer was at the door by the garage,

holding it open. "Come on, come on. What did you do? Miss the bus? Maybe they called off school? You want a ride?"

Sara hadn't thought about having a reason. "We missed the bus, Mr. Demmer. It was all that storm. I brought Petey over," she called.

"Well, come in. Come in. It's nice and warm here. I've got the fireplace going. The wife just saw you coming over here."

Petey was at the door and Sara moved back and called, "Mr. Demmer! I've got to make sure I closed the house. I'll be right back."

"Whoa, Sara, wait," began Mr. Demmer.

But Sara had turned and was running back toward the house.

She heard Petey wail. "Sara!"

She shouted, "I'll be back in a minute. I'll be right back."

She didn't look around but ran back down the road, her shoes making big splashes in the water. She jumped over one of the fallen branches. Her feet were soaked now, making squishes as she ran. And O.P.? She just hoped O.P. wouldn't be soaked.

# 14

The shed door was still open, and as Sara stepped in, she saw that the spattering rain had blown inside and soaked the newspapers and even O.P.'s bed. "O.P.? O.P.?" she called, knowing as she did it that he hadn't returned.

She stood inside the shed, looking out across the yard. The rain dripped off the trees and the roof, splattering on the ground. Small streams burrowed under the pine needles and ran across the sand.

It was not as dark now. The heavy clouds had passed, leaving a grayness and the steady rain. Sara put out a dish of dog food, just in case O.P. came back.

Maybe he had headed for the swamp. The water there would be rising from the storm, as it had that first day she found him. Sara was ready to dash out when she made herself slow down. She had to think. She had to think this time and not go running around frantically.

She shivered. She had to think or she would also be wet and cold quickly. She would search the yard first, as she had done this morning — but now she had to do it carefully.

She knelt down on the ground, pushing her raincoat under her knees, and felt around the edges of the shed. She wouldn't even think of the possibility of the porcupine hiding there. She made herself think of O.P. She moved all the way around the shed and found nothing.

She circled the boat, which already had a lot of water inside of it. She went around the cabin and the woodshed, along the edge of the woods, around the stumps, behind the logs. The rain was soaking through her raincoat, seeping in around the sleeve ends and running down the hood under her chin.

She looked for tracks but the rain had washed everything away. She stopped under one of the big pine trees. There were so many places to look if O.P. was not right here — so many yards, so many sheds, and the woods.

Maybe, before she did all of that, she would try that place in the swamp where she had first seen him. Maybe animals went back to those places. Stories she had read in books said that some did.

The swamp was full of water. There was more than when she'd filled up the water pan for O.P. The log was there, the one she'd walked on before, but it bobbed uneasily under her weight this time. She stepped on the grass on the other side of the creek, and her foot slid into one of the black puddles. But her feet were already so cold and wet that she really didn't feel it.

The rain was still coming down in torrents, splashing everywhere, across her face, down her raincoat, in the water in the swamp. She was bending down to crawl under the alder brush when she thought she heard the sound. A whimper. It sounded like a whimper. Another rush of rain drowned out any sound.

Roots stuck up in the air, and she was sure they were the roots of the tree where she'd first found O.P. Now she clearly heard the cry. It was the cry of O.P. "I'm coming, O.P. I'm coming," she called.

There were big puddles of water, and she heard the sound of her feet in them as she moved toward the tree. She circled around to the far side and there, crouched under the tangle of upended roots, was O.P. He was wet and shivering and crying.

"O.P., I'm here. I made it." Sara reached out and touched the wet fur and gathered up the shivering pup. His black coat was matted and spikey and his wetness made him look thinner than ever.

Sara unzipped her raincoat and held him against her body. O.P.'s shivering stopped momentarily and then continued, harder than ever. Sara held him against her sweater, pulling the raincoat over him to keep out the rain.

"I've got to get you back and get you warmed up," she said. "Oh, I'm so glad I came and found you, O.P." She hugged him close. There was no squirming from the pup, just more shivering.

Sara crawled back around the stump, slower now, clumsily, because of the pup. Her feet moved unsteadily over the mud and the grass and the puddles. Now she could not grab a branch or a bush to steady herself. She needed both hands for O.P.

The log. How was she going to balance herself to cross the log? She'd have to hold O.P. with one hand and hang on to the bushes with the other, or she would slip and they would both go in — and now the creek looked higher than ever. As she put her foot on the log it bobbed, shifting and sliding.

She moved O.P. to her left arm to see if she could hold him with one hand while she steadied herself with the other. O.P. was shivering harder.

Sara started across, putting one foot down, then pulling it back as the log rose up in a swell of water. When it settled, she stepped once more and then grabbed the bushes with her right hand. Her body lurched, but she was on the log. She moved the next foot slowly, and the next, moving her free hand from bush to bush.

The log sank lower and the water swirled around her feet, rushing up around her ankles. A stick, carried by the stream, bumped into the log, causing it to lurch alarmingly. Sara didn't move her feet. She clutched O.P. a little tighter and he squirmed, as if sensing the danger.

"It's all right, O.P. We're almost there," she breathed. Now she moved her foot and then stepped again and once more. Quickly she was across, the wet branch slapping her face as she stepped off the log.

The slap of the branch stung her cheek, and she rubbed wet fingers over it, then forgot it as she felt O.P.'s body tremble. She pulled the raincoat around him. "We're almost there, O.P., and I'll get you nice and warm and dry."

She waded out of the edge of the swamp, right through the puddles. As she came up the knoll that separated the swamp from the yard, she heard the buzz of windshield wipers and saw the lights from Al's truck. It was parked in the yard, near the shed.

Al came around the truck, calling "Sara? Sara? What in God's name are you doing here? Sara?"

Sara pulled the raincoat closer, covering O.P., holding him tight. She stood there in the rain.

Somehow she couldn't think of what to do next. No plan came; no way out. She couldn't run back into the swamp. Al would find O.P.

Al's hoarse voice called again. "My God! Sara! Where have you been? What's going on here?"

He was closer to her, and she could see his frown and the anger in his eyes. There was no place to run, no place to hide.

Now he grabbed her shoulders as if he were going to shake her. "Sara . . . say something. What . . .?"

The raincoat flew open and O.P. shivered, uncontrollably.

"Sara? What is this? This pup? What's going on?"

The rain splattered on Al's mouth and his cheek, and it fell on O.P., who was still shaking in Sara's arm.

"This is O.P., Al — O.P., the orphaned pup," Sara mumbled. The words hardly came out. It was the cold and the rain and the danger of the creek water. Now she started shivering, as hard as O.P.

"Sara, come on. Get in the truck," said Al, grabbing her arm and pushing her forward.

Sara's feet moved, squishy and sodden, and she hugged O.P. tighter. "O.P. . . ." she began.

"Not here," Al commanded. "It's pouring. Get in the truck."

He opened the door and helped her in. There

was a dull thump as the door closed behind her. Then he was around on the other side, sliding in, gunning the engine.

"Sara, I can't believe this. What's going on with you? What will your mom think?" He shook his head as he backed the truck up and turned around.

Sara saw the open shed. "Wait! The dog food," she cried. "O.P. will need the dog food."

"No! Leave it," said Al, curtly, and he pulled out of the yard, leaning forward, trying to see out of the windows that were fogging up.

Leave it. Just leave the dog food and O.P.'s bed and the shed? What would happen to O.P.?

Al was driving into their yard and Sara saw the lights on all over the house. "The electricity must have come back on," she said, numbly.

"Yeah," anwered Al. "I came home to check and Ed Demmer called and said that Petey was there, but you'd run off someplace. I couldn't find you anywhere." He looked at her. "Sara . . ." he began. "Never mind. Let's go in and we'll talk about it there."

Sara sat very still. "What about O.P.?" she asked. She could still feel him trembling under her raincoat.

"O.P.? What is this O.P.? Is it that little scrawny pup you've got?"

The anger was back. Sara could hear it in Al's biting words.

"Well, don't just sit there. You'd better get in and get those wet clothes off," he said, getting out of the truck. "And bring that dog in, too," he added sharply.

Still clutching O.P. in a left arm that was getting tired, Sara followed Al into the house. The radio was blaring and all the lights blazed. After Al hung up his jacket, he went from room to room, turning off lights.

Sara just stood there in the hall with the water dripping off of her coat, making little puddles on the floor. But O.P. had stopped shivering. Maybe he was getting warm from her body.

When Al turned off the radio, it was quiet — very quiet — and he came back to the hall. "Well, don't just stand there. Get that wet stuff off."

"What about O.P.?" Sara asked. "What shall I do about O.P.?"

Al looked at her for a moment, the small frown appearing. Then he reached out and said gruffly, "Here, I'll hold him."

Sara opened the raincoat and handed the wet, furry bundle to Al. O.P. didn't squirm or kick as Al held him carefully, cradling him in his big arms. The pup began to lick his wet fur, stroking with his little tongue.

Al tipped his head, watching. "He looks like a drowned rat. But he's a cute little bugger, isn't he?" He saw Sara looking at him. "Get moving, Sara."

Sara took off the raincoat and slipped off the shoes and socks. She was wet everywhere else, too, her jeans, her sweatshirt, her hair. Then she looked back at Al holding O.P.

"You'd better change the rest of that, too," he said. "He'll be all right. Now, scoot."

Sara hurried into the bedroom, changing quickly, stopping at the bathroom to rub her wet head with a towel. Now what? She had such plans for O.P. She was going to have him trained, to have him ready. What would happen now?

She heard Al's voice from the kitchen. "Bring out something to dry this pup, Sara. See if you can find something, but not one of your mom's good towels."

Sara opened the cupboard where her mom kept the cleaning things and found an old piece of towel. She took it out to the kitchen where Al was sitting with the pup in his lap.

He reached for the towel. "Are you sure this is an old one?"

Sara nodded.

Al took the towel and gently rubbed O.P., soaking up the bits of moisture, tousling the black fur. "There, that's better," he said, giving a final wipe. He gave the towel back to Sara.

"Now, he should probably have something to eat," said Al. "Let's see, maybe some warm milk and bread. You'd better warm the milk a little. Just put it in a pan." Al was stroking the pup with his big hand.

Sara moved about the kitchen, getting everything ready. Al still hadn't said anything about O.P., about where he came from, about what she was doing with him. But Sara was sure that would be coming — and soon.

She poured the milk over the bread and carried the dish to where Al was sitting with O.P.

"Now, spread some newspapers on the floor and we'll put the food dish here," said Al.

Sara found the paper and put it down, just as she had in the shed, and placed the bowl on it. Al set O.P. down and the pup attacked the food greedily, the way he always did. Sara sat back on the floor and watched. Al stood up and then disappeared, without saying anything.

O.P. finished the food, licking the dish, and Sara held it so it wouldn't slide all over. O.P. braced himself on his legs and put his head up, sniffling and smelling.

"Strange place, isn't it, O.P.?" said Sara. "Different than your shed." She moved her hand toward him and he ran off, shying away. This time she put her hand around him and pulled him close, across her lap. He lay there but still put his head up in the sniffing way.

"New smells, O.P.?" Sara stroked him, feeling that the once wet fur was now only damp.

Al was back with a box, a much larger one than the one Sara had used in the shed. He placed it on the floor and found some newspapers and spread them in the bottom. "Now, put him in here," he said. "And get another old dry towel to put in here for a bed."

Sara followed his directions, easing O.P. down in the box, watching him look around at yet another strange place.

Sara got the old towel out of the cupboard. It was coming now. Whatever would happen to her — and to O.P. — was coming. What could she say? How could she get Al to let her keep O.P.? Her plan had been to get him ready to be a good dog, but there was no time for that now.

She put the towel down in the box, and O.P. sniffed it and pulled it a little before he lay down, closing his eyes. Sara wanted to say all the words she always said to O.P. about being tired and going to sleep. But they wouldn't come out, not with Al watching.

Al moved to set the coffeepot on the stove and to get a cup. "Sit down, Sara," he said. The frown was back on his face.

# 15

Sara sat in the kitchen chair. She could see O.P. curled up in the box and she was scared. She couldn't give him up now, not after she'd taken care of him and lost him and found him. She'd just say she didn't want a horse, not ever. She'd just take O.P., even if Petey was getting a dog.

Petey. Maybe it would be easier if he was here. She had always thought of herself as sitting and talking with her father — Al — like this. But now it scared her.

Al slid into the chair on the other side of the table, setting his coffee cup down.

"Where's Petey? Maybe we should get Petey," said Sara.

Al curled his hands around the steaming cup. "Later. I think we'd better talk about this pup, the dog. Then I'll pick up Petey later."

Sara pushed back her damp hair, tucking it behind her ears. Her mom wasn't there. Before, her mom had always been here. She looked at Al.

"Well . . ." he said. "I think you'd better start by telling me the story."

Sara did, slowly at first, then quickly, as she told him how she found O.P. and about Patchy getting killed and then putting O.P. in the shed and caring for him and pulling out the quills and losing him early in the morning and finding him. She finished and looked out the window.

The rain had stopped. It was not pouring over the eaves and falling into the puddles.

Al's fingers tapped the table. "And when you said you were jogging or doing your homework, you were really feeding the pup?" he asked.

Sara looked back at him. "Yes."

He sat back, putting his hand under his chin. He had the small frown above his eyes.

"I . . . I didn't really mean to lie. I really did those things," said Sara.

He looked at her questioningly, and she faltered. "Well, I did other things, too. And I guess I just didn't say anything about them. A lot of things were only partly true."

"Why?" he asked. "Why didn't you say something to us? To your mom, if not to me?" His arm made a thumping sound as he dropped it against the table.

"I was afraid you wouldn't like O.P. because he wasn't a good dog. Patchy was half-wild, you said."

135

She had to bite her lip because she was close to tears. "I was going to keep O.P. and train him so he could do all the things that would make him a good dog — a dog you would like."

Al pushed his chair back. Finally he said, "Sara . . . Sara, I wish your mother was here."

She nodded. "And I wish Petey was here, too."

He sat there for a minute. Then he reached across the table and curled his big hand over hers. "But they're not here. I guess it's just you and me. I always thought it would be nice to have a daughter and watch her grow up and then . . . then it seemed it wasn't so easy to be a father to you."

Sara nodded again. "I know what you mean, Al. I thought about all the things like jogging and fishing. I really liked the fishing."

This time he smiled, just a little, and he said, "It's this dog thing. I guess I'd better tell you about that."

He moved his hand back to the coffee cup, running his fingers around the rim and back and forth on the handle. "You see, when I was little, like Petey, I lived in a place that looked a lot like Boettcher's. It was such a mess. Cars all over, junk all around. And the kids teased me. They called me "Junker Al" and "Al the Junkman." I hated it. But my dad was in the junk business. That's how he made his living. You would come driving down the road and then you could see our place for miles — because of all the junked cars around the yard and in the field. That's all you saw. I promised myself I would never have a place like that when I grew up. I would have it nice — as nice as I could possibly have it."

"The best," murmured Sara.

He stopped moving his fingers and looked sharply at her before he looked away. "Yeah, the best. I suppose that's the way it sounded to others. I guess I always just thought of it as good." He moved in his chair, stretching out his legs. "I guess what I'm trying to say is . . . I'm sorry about this dog thing, that you thought the pup had to be trained, perfect, whatever. We would have taken that pup in, this O.P. I'm not that hardhearted."

He sat up again, turning toward her. "Or am I, Sara? Do I seem that way?"

Sara was uncomfortable. "No. I guess . . . I guess it was easier for me not to say anything and to wait and to hope for something. I didn't know about these things like the junkyard when you were little."

Al shook his head. "And I didn't tell them, either. I always told the other stories."

"They were good stories, Al," said Sara.

"You mean you heard them?" he asked, surprised. "It seemed to me you always had your nose in a book when I was telling Petey a story."

Sara edged her fingers along the table. "Well . . . not always, Al. I listened and I heard them — and I liked them, too."

There was silence. Sara could hear the clock ticking and then O.P. stirred in his bed, bumping the box.

Al smiled. "And now there's O.P. Why did you call him O.P.?" he asked.

"O.P. — for orphaned pup," answered Sara.

"Well, I think we should get this orphaned pup a home," said Al. "A home with us."

Sara looked up, watchful. "Do you mean he can stay, Al?" she asked.

He came around the table and knelt alongside her chair, sliding his arm around her, looking at the sleeping pup. "Of course he can stay. He'll be part of the family."

Sara put her head down against his shoulder. "Thanks, Al. Oh, thanks, Al," she said.

"Hey, your hair is still all wet," he said, standing up. "And I think I had better get Petey, or Mr. Demmer will be looking for both of us. And a little later we'll go back to the shed and clean up and we'll also have to tell the owners that you used it. I'll talk to the Boettchers, too. We'll work something out there."

Sara nodded in agreement as Al left the kitchen.

She sat back in her chair. It was just like a maze. When you thought you couldn't get out and had to go all the way back, suddenly, there you were — at the end and out. The secret was gone and now she could have O.P. here and play with him and watch him. And Al. Maybe it wouldn't be so hard with Al now. They could go jogging and he could teach her how to take care of a dog, how to really take care of him. Maybe Al was right. Maybe she did have to get wet — and grow up a little.

Sara heard Petey's excited voice. "You mean Sara really has a pup, Al? A real, live pup?"

Then he was bursting into the house, coming into the kitchen. "Where is he, Sara? Where is the puppy?"

Sara pointed to the box and put her finger to her lip. "Shh, Petey. He's in there," she whispered. "Sleeping."

O.P. rolled over and blinked and then curled up the opposite way and went back to sleep again.

"Boy, he's a beauty." Petey's whisper was loud. "Pretty, isn't he?"

Al stood in the doorway. "And I told him you'd tell him the whole story, Sara."

"Will you, Sara? Will you tell me the story?" asked Petey.

Sara nodded. "I'll tell you the story of O.P. — Orphaned Pup."

## About the Author

ELEANOR J. LAPP is the author of several picture books, including *The Blueberry Bears*. She is an elementary school teacher and lives in Land O' Lakes, Wisconsin. This is her first novel.